MEMBERS ONLY

For more information about the author and her books, visit
her website— www.shanteltessier.com
You can join her reader group. It's the only place to get
exclusive teasers, first to know about current projects and
release dates. And also have chances to win some amazing
giveaways- Shantel's Sinful Side

Editor: Amanda Rash
Formatter: Melissa Cunningham
Cover Designer: Shanoff Designs

CODE OF SILENCE

THE DARK KINGDOM

PROLOGUE

LUCA

Ten years old

"WHO DID YOU fucking talk to?" my father demands.

"No one, John," Uncle Marco snaps. "You know that—"

"I know what I've been told and what you are saying doesn't add up!" He pokes his brother in the chest. "And you." He points at my aunt who stands in the corner of the living room with her back against the window that overlooks their backyard. "You've been running your fucking mouth too much."

Tears fill her brown eyes as she stares at my father. Her shoulders shake, and she bites her bottom lip, trying to swallow a sob.

John Bianchi puts the fear of God in you. Because he is god. As the Don—the ringleader of the Italian-American

1

Mafia—he decides when your time is up and how you pay for your sins. He was born in New York, but he and my uncle moved to Las Vegas when my father was fourteen. Uncle Marco was twelve. The laws in Sin City were more fluid back then, so my father was able to get his hands dirtier. He likes life messy.

"Don't talk to her like that!" Marco shoves my father.

"I'll talk to the bitch however I fucking please!" He punches my uncle, knocking him to his knees.

Aunt Ava cries out as blood runs down his chin, but she doesn't dare go to her husband. No, she stays in her corner, knowing damn well there's nothing she can do. At this point, all she can hope is that my father spares her life.

"You son of a bitch," Marco growls, wiping the blood off.

My father pulls the gun from the waistband of his dress slacks and points it down at his brother.

"John!" He throws up his hands, eyes so dark they're almost black, pleading with my father to spare his life. "Come on. We'll figure this out. I swear it wasn't me ..."

My father pulls the trigger.

I jump, momentarily deafened by the sound except for the ringing in my ears. Ava cries out, falling to the floor. Bringing her knees to her chest, she openly sobs.

I look back at my uncle. He never did live up to the expectations of the Bianchi family. My father was born in the mafia, and he will die in it, but his younger brother always played a role. Marco has wanted out for years, and this was the only way he was going to get it. Putting a bullet in his head was John Bianchi's way of sparing him. He could have made my uncle suffer.

He turns to face my aunt. "No!" she screams. "Please

..." She shakes violently as tears run down her face, smearing the makeup she put on earlier. It's their anniversary. We caught them on their way out to dinner to celebrate fifteen years of marriage.

"Strip," my father orders.

"Please!" She sobs, shaking her head.

"Remove your dress. Now!" he shouts.

Using the window for support, she slowly gets to her feet. With shaky hands, she undoes the hook that holds her dress around her neck. It falls down her chest, stomach, and hips before pooling around her black heels. Her frail body shakes as she covers her bare breasts with her arms.

My father smiles at her, obviously happy with what he sees. Or what he doesn't see. A wire. Someone has been feeding information to the feds, and he suspects it's her. But the things that have gotten back to my father were spot-on, so if she wasn't the snitch, then her husband was.

He walks over to her, grips her auburn hair, and jerks her head back. Placing the gun under her chin, he shows no emotion as she closes her eyes and sobs uncontrollably. "You keep your goddamn mouth shut; do you understand me?"

She begins to nod, but he shoves her head back farther with the barrel of the gun.

"Fucking say it, Ava!" he growls in her face.

"Keep ... my ... mouth ... shut," she chokes out.

He releases her, and she cries out when he shoves her to the floor once again. Turning to face me, he places his gun back in his waistband. Coming over to me, he says, "Never let anyone stand in your way, son. Not even fucking blood. They'll be the first to undercut you, and they should be the first to die for it."

Twenty-two years old

THE MORNING AIR IS COOL ON MY SKIN. THE HARSH wind whistling as it blows through the tall trees on this mountainside. The sun is just starting to rise on this glorious Friday. My heart pounds with adrenaline.

Anticipation.

The sound of screaming is like music to my ears. A beacon of hope calling to me, letting me know I'm close to my destination. But as much as I like the sound, I don't need it. I know where he is because I set the traps.

A week ago, my father called me to his home office in New York and ordered me to go *hunting*. But this isn't the kind of hunt where you hang your kill on the wall as a trophy to impress others. No, this is the kind you let the wild animals feast on and then leave to rot once you've trapped your prey.

I come to the clearing and see a man by the name of Bernard lying on the ground. He looks up as I approach with my two men. His lips pull back in a snarl, and drool runs down his chin like a rabid dog. Seems fitting since he's on a leash.

"You!" Spit flies out of his mouth. His eyes go to Nite, who stops beside me. "You will pay for this!"

He's not lying. The life of the Cosa Nostra is an endless circle of revenge. It's something we all came to terms with long ago. Every one of us understands that you live one day just to possibly be killed the next. But in this day and age, it's not just limited to the mafioso. There are too many angry people in the world who feel they have the right to take your life.

I take a step toward him. He tries to crawl away, but the

teeth from the bear trap bite into his leg, preventing it. Gritting his teeth, he throws his head back in pain. His veins protrude from his neck, and the spit flies as he pants.

"Would you like me to set you free?" I ask, watching the puddle of blood grow underneath him. I was taught to play with my food. Sometimes the mind game fucks them up more than the actual violence.

"Fuck you, Luca!" he growls.

"What do you think, Nite?" I look over at the man who stands next to me. His hands are tightly fisted, and his shoulders shake with fury, but he says nothing. He turns to me, his green eyes almost glowing with rage.

"I agree." I nod as if I can read his mind. "I think we should give him a fighting chance."

It's all about the hunt. That's what makes this so exciting and gets my blood pumping. I was raised on violence.

Plus, my father sent me to do a job, and I won't fail him. If I do, I'll be the one in a trap. And I refuse to give him any reason not to need me. Useless men end up dead and buried in the desert. My father doesn't show favoritism, not even to his own sons. You either kill or get killed. It's the Bianchi way.

The man yanks on the chain that secures the bear trap into the dirt. He won't be able to get it out. I set all twenty traps out here myself. We raided their log cabin an hour ago, entering from the front to push the fuckers out through the back, knowing they would try to escape through these woods.

And we were ready. We spent all of last night getting things in order.

Reaching down, I grab the knife out of my black boot

and lift it in the air. Bernard raises his hands to shield himself, thinking I'm going to throw it at his face. As if I would give him that kind of mercy. Instead, it lands blade down in the dirt next to his bloody leg. "Start cutting," I order.

"Wh ... what?" he cries and yanks it from the ground. "This won't cut through the chain." He seethes, shaking it at me.

"It won't." I agree with him.

His eyes widen once he understands what I'm saying. "I'm not going to cut my leg off!" he shouts.

I look back over at Oliver Nite. The man has been a member of the Bianchi family for fifteen years now. My father found him fighting off a group of thugs trying to steal what little he had. He took Nite in because he saw an opportunity. One—he could fight. And two—he was a child who had no one. My father could use the boy to his advantage. "What do you think?" I ask him.

He takes a step toward the man.

"Stay back!" Bernard orders, lifting the knife that I gave him to cut through his leg. His only chance to free himself from the trap. His only chance at freedom.

I throw my head back, laughing.

"I mean it!" he screams. "I already cut you once. I'll do it again." He swings the knife around aimlessly in the air.

Nite goes to him, gripping Bernard's wrist and squeezing so hard that he releases the knife with a cry.

"Pathetic," I spit.

As a member of the Mafia, you are trained for situations like this. And this guy has apparently forgotten all his beatings. I never will.

"Luca?"

I turn to face my father's right-hand man, Diaz. He

made it sound as though I needed the protection, but we all knew Diaz was sent to spy. To report back to my father how I did and whether I passed the test.

He holds his finger to his earpiece. "We have another one. Snake pit, sir."

I smile. The snake pit is another trap I set for these sorry bastards. A ten-foot-deep hole that I had my men dig last night, then place five snakes in. None of them venomous. I wanted them captured and scared, not dead. "Tell them to take him back to the cabin." Then I turn back to the man. "We're going to wrap this up."

Diaz hands me a pair of Lineman's pliers and a razor blade. "Nite, you may do the honors." I pass him the razor blade. He stares down at it, his eyes glazing over with excitement. I watch the vein in his neck throb with anticipation.

Payback is sweet. And bloody.

Walking over to Bernard, I grab his arms and pull him toward me. He screams out as the chain on the bear trap pulls taut, stretching his body. Falling to my knees at his head, I order, "Open your mouth."

He clamps it shut, brown eyes glaring up at me. They promise retribution. He knows his hours are numbered, but he also knows his men will retaliate. It's just a matter of when, so I'm going to make it worth it.

"Nite," I call out.

He stomps on Bernard's trapped leg, and the man screams out in agony. I use the opportunity to reach into his mouth and grab his tongue with the pliers. He mumbles a few choice words and tries to shake his head. His tongue instantly begins to bleed when I squeeze, securing the grip. His arms flail around, trying to push me away, but he is unsuccessful.

I look up at Nite as he bends down next to me. And

without a second thought, he takes the razor blade and slices it through Bernard's tongue, cutting it off.

I stand, the pliers still in my hand and his tongue hanging on the end. Bernard thrashes on the ground as blood gushes from his mouth. The sounds of gurgling and vomiting follow.

I hand the pliers to Nite, and he stares at it as if it's his firstborn. The most prized possession he'll ever own.

"We could make him swallow it," I offer.

Nite shakes his head and hands it to Diaz to hold.

"Good idea. Keep it as a souvenir." I pick up the knife from the ground. "You had your chance at freedom. You should have taken it." I place it back in my boot. Bernard lies there. He's twisted around to where he's on his hands, his mouth wide open as the blood continues to run down his chin and cover his shirt along with the ground. His body shakes, his leg yanking on the bear trap and causing the chain to clank. His skin is so torn up, you can see the tendon and muscles.

"Diaz?" I snap my fingers, and he hands me the ice chest.

I bend down, opening the small red cooler. Most of the ice has melted, leaving it full of water and a white washcloth. I make sure to dunk it into the freezing water and turn to Bernard. I kick his shoulder, pushing him onto his back, and straddle his chest. He fights me, but again, he's unsuccessful as I cram the washcloth into his bloody mouth. "We need to apply pressure," I tell him while he tries to breathe. Blood sprays me from around the corners of his mouth as he coughs and chokes on the water. His body convulses while trying to breathe. "To make the bleeding stop."

His hands slap at my body aimlessly. I stand and step away from him. His shaky hands yank the washcloth out and throw it to the ground before he grabs at his blood covered chest and neck.

I snort, watching his sorry ass flop around like a fish out of water. I turn, giving him my back, because I'm done playing with him. I get bored easily. "Boys, shall we?"

We walk off, leaving the man behind us with his leg in the trap and bleeding from his mouth. An animal will smell the blood, and he'll either be eaten alive, or he'll eventually die from blood loss or dehydration. Either way will be painful.

Nite slaps me on the back.

"You okay?" I ask, giving him a quick glance.

This week has been rough for him, and I hate it. I've always looked up to him like an older brother. And he's the reason we're five hundred miles away from home to begin with.

He nods because, well, that's all he does. That sorry bastard we just walked away from cut out Nite's tongue seven days ago because he wouldn't give up intel on my family.

We're the Bianchis, the Italian-American Mafia who runs most of Las Vegas. We've all got bounties on our heads and are always a target. If you don't take out your enemies, they will take you out first.

The Mafia is the world's most exclusive men's club, and once you're in, you're in for life. Nite and I both wear the ring on our right hand. It's gold and big. Heavy. The thing is tacky, but it represents power. Nite is the only Bianchi who wears the ring that wasn't born into the family. My parents adopted him soon after my father found him, making him

9

Oliver Nite Bianchi for life. So, like me, death is his only way out.

I didn't have a choice. Twenty-two years ago, I was born into it, and I've been proving my worth and loyalty to my father and his men ever since. This trip will not be any different. I made this trip to show my loyalty to Nite as he has shown to me and my family. Heads will roll. Literally. And it'll be by my bloodstained hands.

HAVEN

I WALK DOWN the hallway, my books in one hand and my cell in the other. Luca hasn't sent me a text in days. I hate when he does this—goes off the grid—and he's been doing it more and more lately. And I don't just mean with me. He's avoided his classes as well. It's his father. I know it. His family is ... different. They're the dark figures who hide in the back alleys, just waiting for you to pass by. If you have something they want, they take it, no questions asked. He's treating his senior year of college no different than anything else—like an inconvenience. And all the staff and faculty turn a blind eye. They don't care. They get paid to teach our ungrateful, spoiled asses. Why should they give a fuck who shows and who doesn't?

"Hey, you girls wanna help me out with something tonight?" Jasmine asks. Skipping beside me, she runs her hand along the dark blue wall where *Wildcats* is painted in white. She's in a cheerful mood today for a girl who got dumped last night via text message.

"No thanks." Emilee laughs from my other side. "I'm not in the mood to spend the night in jail. I have plans this weekend with my parents."

Jasmine rolls her eyes. "It's harmless."

"I'll help," I say. Not like I have anything else going on. I would normally spend my evening with Luca, but it's obvious I'll be available tonight. And every other night to come until he decides to pick up his damn phone and send me a text.

"See ..." She throws her arm over my shoulders and looks at Emilee. "That was the correct response when a friend asks you a question like that. We're supposed to be ride or die bitches. I got your back, and you got mine."

Emilee snorts. "Last time I had your *back*, we all ended up in the back of a squad car."

Jasmine pulls away from me. "I talked us out of getting arrested." She waves her off.

"No, your father did because he's friends with the mayor," Emilee retorts.

"You gotta admit those handcuffs turned you on." Jasmine wiggles her dark eyebrows.

"You have major issues." Emilee sighs.

I check my phone again. *Still nothing.* I grip it tighter, my annoyance growing with every passing second. Why hasn't he responded to my texts? It doesn't take more than a second to send a fucking message. I need something to take my mind off it.

"What do you have planned?" I get Jasmine back on track. Emilee is right; she has issues, and we don't have time to go through them.

"I'm gonna slash Trenton's tires," she answers, twirling her bleach blond hair around her pointer finger. "Maybe bust out some windows. Depends on how much I drink before we go."

I snort. "Why waste your time? You know he'll have whatever you do to his precious car fixed tomorrow."

She holds up her pointer finger. "Doubtful. Pretty boy

doesn't have a job, and he's already in deep shit with his *daddy* for getting kicked off the football team." She presses her thumb to her nose and sniffs. "For them finding that stash of coke in his locker."

"And who alerted Coach to his stash?" Emilee asks, raising a brow.

Jasmine gives her an innocent smile, showing off her pearly whites. "It was anonymous."

"Sure, it was." She snorts.

"I'm in." The bastard deserves to spend a few days stuck at home for how he did her. Dirty. I'm in the mood to dish out some karma, and since I can't give it to the boy who deserves it, Trenton's a good second choice. We both look at Emilee.

She sighs, giving in. "Yeah, yeah."

"Great." Jasmine starts to walk backward, but as she goes to pass the men's bathroom, the door flies open, knocking her forward.

Cross, a member of the Dark Kings, comes barging out of it with his hands shoved in the pockets of his ripped jeans. He wears a backward black hat and a Wildcats hoodie. All the players on the Wildcats baseball team have one.

"Excuse you," Jasmine calls out.

He ignores us and continues to walk down the hall and toward the back door exit that leads to the baseball fields. Practice starts in thirty minutes. His chiseled face a mixed mask of annoyance and pissed.

"Fucker," she calls out, flipping him off behind his back.

Emilee sighs. "Are you just trying to get into trouble today?"

"What? That idiot hit me with the door." She rubs her ass.

"He's a member of the Dark Kings," Emilee whispers, her eyes darting around the now empty hallway.

Jasmine scoffs. "I don't bow to anyone. And just 'cause you suck a King's dick doesn't mean I gotta kiss one's ass."

I hang my head. "Can we get back on track—"

"I gotta go," Jasmine interrupts me. "But yeah, I'll pick you both up a little after ten. Be ready and wear all black. Don't wanna be seen. And don't worry about the supplies. I got you covered." Then she walks down the hallway and out the double doors, heading home for the day.

"Why are we wasting our time? You know she'll be back with him tomorrow when he calls to cuss her out for what we do tonight." Emilee sighs.

"Have anything better to do?" I ask.

She goes to answer, but a phone goes off.

My heart races as I look down at mine in my hand, hoping it's Luca.

"Ugh." She stomps her foot when she realizes it's hers.

My teeth grind. *Why do I do this?* Why do I allow him to get me this worked up? Why do I care so much when it's very clear he does not?

Ping. Ping.

"Who the hell is blowing up your phone?" I ask frustrated. "Your mother?"

Her parents are very strict. They don't know just how wild their little girl is. She's always pretended to be the innocent one in our tight circle. Even now, as a sophomore in college, she waits until they go to bed and then sneaks out to all the parties. I don't know how she hasn't been caught yet. I've had my mom lie to cover for her before. Jasmine's too. Eventually, her mother is gonna catch on and ban her from hanging out with us.

Ping. Ping.

13

We come to a stop, and she shoves her books into my chest. I let out a puff of air, trying not to drop them along with my own.

"Who the hell knows." She growls, dropping her backpack to the floor and digging her phone out of the side pocket.

Ping.

"It's Bones." She sighs as her blue eyes run over the screen.

"Of course, it is." I roll mine. She can get her fuckboy to message her, but I can't get the guy I love to even acknowledge me.

She throws her backpack over one shoulder and types away. "He wants me to go meet him before baseball practice starts."

"For a quickie?" I question. "E, you have to stop jumping on that. You're at his beck and call every minute of the day." I have never seen a girl so dick whipped. It's actually pathetic. And the truth is, she doesn't even love the guy. She is just that obsessed with his cock. And him with her pussy.

Her blue eyes pin me with a challenge, and I stiffen, knowing what's coming. "Do you wanna be the pot or the kettle?"

Her words make me hate Luca Bianchi even more. Damn him. "It's different."

"Explain it to me." She arches a perfectly dark brow while pushing a hip out.

I can't.

The only difference is that I love the guy who uses me.

Sighing, she adds, "I'm sorry, I ..."

"It's okay." I wave her off. It's not her fault I'm pissy. Or that Luca has forgotten about me.

14

She bites her pink painted bottom lip. Her blue eyes drop back down to look at her phone, and I see her fighting the battle of telling him to go to hell or meeting him to fuck his brains out.

"His dick can't be that good," I argue.

She rips her books from my arms. "He's going through a lot right now."

Bones is ... for lack of a better word, a fucking prick! Everyone knows him and his three friends as the Dark Kings, and they're all fucking arrogant pieces of shit. Titan, Cross, and Bones are all seniors this year with Luca. Grave, Bones's younger brother, is a junior. The Kings are just like Luca—going to take over for their fathers and rule the world. Emilee, Jasmine, and I chose to stay because we didn't want to leave each other behind. We knew that day would come eventually, but we're trying to put it off for as long as we can.

"And your pussy is his therapist?" I ask.

Ping.

"I gotta go." She storms down the hall, her mind made up. The pinging fades as she leaves me to go meet him in the men's locker room to suck his dick.

With a sigh, I grab the black leather strap to my white Louis Vuitton Discovery backpack and turn the corner, heading to the library. Most students are done for the day, but I stay late on Fridays to do an hour tutoring session. I've always made straight A's. And when the school year started, I found a few kids in my classes weren't quite ready for the curriculum, so I offered to tutor them.

I walk up the first flight of stairs, my black leather Louboutin Mary Janes clapping on the white tile. Turning the corner, I proceed up the next, when a book slips from my grasp. It tumbles down the steps, making a loud slapping noise that bounces off the abandoned hallways. "Shit." I run after it. I bend down to pick it up, but someone beats me to it. I look up from my crouched position at the man who stands before me. He holds my book in one hand and his cell in the other.

I stand and rip my book from his grip. "Nice to see you haven't lost your phone." Then I turn and start to walk away from him, stomping my heels up the second set of stairs.

"Haven ..." He grabs my upper arm, pulling me to a stop.

I spin around to face him, yanking out of his hold. "Don't you start."

"I didn't have any cell service where I was," he explains, his big dark eyes pleading for me to forgive him.

I don't.

But now I know he was out in the desert or the woods somewhere. Probably helping his father bury a body. Or two. His father considers that as close to bonding as they will ever get. But what do you expect when your dad is a Don; the ringleader of the Italian-American Mafia?

I wish that had deterred me from falling in love with him. Sadly, when I found out, I was already too far in. That's the scary thing about love; it blurs the lines of right and wrong. You choose to ignore what you should question because it's dangerous and thrilling at the same time.

"How long have you been back?" I demand.

Walking up the three stairs, he closes the distance between us, forcing me to look up at him even though he stands on the step below me. He hates people looking down at him for any reason. Reaching up, he pulls the strap of my backpack off my shoulder.

I go to pick it up. "Luca ..."

But he grabs my arm, stopping me from bending down. "An hour." He answers my previous question and cups my face with his warm hand. My breath starts to quicken. The feeling in my chest has my thighs tightening.

No! I will not allow him to do this to me.

"I knew you had tutoring, so I came straight here to see you."

As I look over his freshly shaven face, I know he's showered recently. I can still smell the lingering citrus of his bodywash on his flawless skin. The guy is too gorgeous to be real. It's truly unfair. He has his father's jet-black hair. Normally, he wears it spiked and shorter on the sides, but right now, he has it combed back. And he has dark eyes, but not as dark as his father's or his brother's. They're framed with long dark lashes. A chiseled jaw. Dressed in a black fitted T-shirt and dark jeans, he looks utterly delicious.

His late grandfather was from Italy, but his father was born in New York and lived there until he moved to Vegas when he was fourteen. Where Mr. Bianchi met Luca's mother. Her father owned a very large concrete company, and concrete is useful when you have bodies that can be hidden under the new foundations being poured daily. No one has ever come out and told me, but I connected the dots. His father wanted access to the properties to hide evidence and bodies, and he got it when he married Luca's mother. I've done my research on the Mafia; they marry for power. In some cases, that even means marrying blood relatives. But his father moved back to New York when Luca was ten, leaving Luca and his brothers here. He knew they would do his bidding in Vegas while he was able to control New York. He was able to cover more ground that way. All part of his plan to take over the world.

He wraps his free hand around my waist and pulls me to him. I don't pull away. Fuck, I'm just as bad as Emilee.

Dick whipped.

Good dick will make a girl stupid. I should become a lesbian.

"I have to go," I tell him but make no move to pull away.

"Cancel," he whispers, his lips inches from mine. My heart begins to beat faster, knowing he wants to spend time with me.

You stupid bitch. "I can't ..."

"Yes, you can." His head dips to my neck, and he kisses the tender spot behind my ear. My head falls back, and I moan but cut it off in case any classmates are lingering. "I've missed you." He licks up my neck to the shell of my ear. "I thought about you the entire time I was gone." His voice drops to a growl, and I feel his hard cock against my lower stomach when he rubs his hips against me.

"Lie ..." I breathe but so badly wish it was the truth.

His hand travels up my back and fists my hair. I wore it down today in hopes that I would see him. "I pulled up that naughty picture I took of you last week." *Oh, shit.* "The one where you're lying on my bed naked with your hand between your legs. I stroked my cock thinking of you."

"Luca." I pant. *Please don't stop.*

"I pictured you on your knees while I fucked your mouth ..."

I whimper. That's his favorite. He loves it when I give him head. He says I'm the best, but I call bullshit. It's not that hard to open your mouth and let a guy fuck it. It doesn't take any actual talent. But then again, I've never had a dick, so I guess not all girls suck the same. I did have a friend who couldn't lick a lollipop more than five times before she would just bite it to pieces. I wonder if that's how she gives head?

His free hand slides up my side to my chest. Dipping into my crimson V-neck shirt, he squeezes my breasts over my bra. I want him to rip the constricting fabric off. "And I imagined you on your hands and knees while I fucked that pretty little cunt from behind."

My hands grip his black fitted T-shirt. My thighs tighten when he talks to me that way. He has a filthy mouth in and out of the bedroom. It's one thing I've always liked about him. I'm not as prissy and uptight as the kids at this college think.

HIS MOUTH IS ON MINE. MY BACK IS PRESSED INTO THE *rock wall. Nightfall covers us in darkness. I don't care. All I can think about is him. All I can feel is him. And all I want is him.*

"Please, Luca?" I pull away, panting.

His hands trail down my shirt and over to my ribs. They burn like my insides. My entire body is on fire. "You sure you're ready?" he asks as his lips kiss my neck.

"Yes." My hands grip his shirt, yanking him closer to me. I can't get him close enough.

He reaches for the hem of my shirt and rips it over my head. I almost cry as the hot air hits my bare skin. I don't have a bra on, and my nipples ache as they rub against the fabric of his shirt.

"Fuck, I've wanted you for so long ..." He trails off, and then I feel his lips on my nipples.

I gasp and dig my hands into his hair. Thrusting my head back, I bang my head on the rock and close my eyes. His hands go to my jean shorts, and I help him shove them along with my underwear down my legs.

His hands go to my naked thighs, and my legs shake. "Nervous, baby?"

I can hear the amusement in his question. I'm a virgin, and I'm very aware that he isn't. I could kill that bitch Lucy Bellinger for fucking him. She took what I wanted. He never really dated her, but they hooked up. Over and over again. Her dad is friends with his, and they're always over at his house, so it was bound to happen. Typical story—he used her, and she fell for him. But that was two years ago. She moved away, and somehow, he noticed me. We've been seeing each other for a month now, and although that's not much time, I've known him all my life. I've wanted him for years. Now is my chance, and I'm not going to let it go.

"No," I growl and undo his jeans.

"I'm going to fuck you right here," he warns me. As if I should be scared.

"Yes." I'm not.

He finds my hands and shoves them above my head, pinning them to the rock in one of his. I whimper, pushing my hips into his.

His free hand reaches between our bodies and moves between my legs. He cups my pussy before sliding a finger into me.

"Luca ..." I gasp his name, the sensation making heat run up my spine.

"Fuck, you're wet, Haven," he growls, lowering his head to my neck. "And so fucking tight. Your pussy is going to feel so good."

I pump my hips, not really knowing what I'm doing but needing more. "Please?" I beg.

He removes his finger, and then I feel the head of his cock

rub against me. Just when I think I can't take anymore, he pushes into me.

I scream out into the dark night as he stretches me, and a burning sensation rips through me.

He slaps his now free hand over my mouth, pressing my body into the rock wall. It's the only thing that shields us from my parents' house. My hands fight with his to release me, but he holds them prisoner above my head.

"Shh," he whispers, his hot breath hitting my face. The moon shines down on us, making his dark eyes shine. They bore into mine intently, hungrily, causing my pussy to tighten. "You wanted it. Now take it."

I WILLINGLY GAVE HIM MY VIRGINITY. OUR FIRST TIME wasn't slow and sweet because that's not him. It's not me. I like when he hurts me. When he chokes me. Or when he rips my shirt, throws me on the bed, and fucks me until I can't walk. He takes great pleasure in making my body weak.

My pussy clenches at the thought, knowing how rough he'll be since it's been a few days. He's always the most barbaric after he comes back from a *job* with his father. I used to try to get him to tell me what he did, but he never discloses that information, so I gave up asking.

"I imagined your nails scraping down my back. Your heels digging into my ass. Speaking of ass ..." His hand cups it and lifts me off my feet.

I shriek in surprise as he slams my back into the wall next to the window that overlooks the courtyard. I wrap my legs around his narrow hips and hook my heels together. Then his lips are on mine. His tongue forces its way into my mouth, and I welcome it. My hips grind into his, and my hands go to his dark, luscious hair, gripping and pulling. He growls into my mouth before pulling away quickly, leaving my lips feeling swollen and bruised. My underwear instantly soaked.

His dark eyes look down into mine, and he licks his wet lips. "Cancel," he repeats, now panting. "Tell me I can spend the rest of the day drowning in that pussy of yours."

ONE

HAVEN

Four years later

THE MORNING LAS Vegas sun beats down on me. Sweat covers my face, neck, and chest along with the rest of my body. "Garden" by Halsey blares in my ears from my wireless earbuds. My phone strapped to my upper arm.

My feet pound the ground as I push myself, knowing I don't have much farther to go. This is my morning ritual; wake up, drink a cup of coffee, and then run until I feel like I'm dying. It helps clear my mind and keeps me in shape.

I see the old stone and stucco mansion come into view at the end of the two-lane road in the exclusive neighborhood. I'm sucking in breath after breath, and my sides burn, but I push harder. Faster. My thighs scream, and my feet hurt, but I don't quit. I'm too close. My once tight ponytail has come loose, and strands hang down around my face, sticking to my sweat-covered neck and chest. It makes my skin itch.

My mind wanders, thinking about where I am in my life

right now and why I'm still stuck here in Sin City. At twenty-four years old, I'm currently living with my parents and trying to get my train wreck of a life back on track. I'm what most would call a fucking mess. But am I supposed to have my life figured out at my age? I've heard stories from others that you're expected to go crazy in your twenties, to party and sleep around. If you ask the right people, they'd say I'm on the right track.

Nearing the end of the road, I take a hard right through the open gate, and the sight of a black Bugatti La Voiture Noire makes me stumble.

As if my legs trip over an imaginary rope, I fall on the driveway, my knees hitting the hot concrete first. Then I drop to my side, rolling a few times from the momentum. "Motherfucker!" I hiss, yanking the damn earbuds from my ears.

Looking over at the car sitting in my parents' driveway, I feel like a hurricane is about to destroy everything in my life without any warning. No time to board up my feelings and hide away from what I know will be catastrophic to my psyche.

Nothing involving that car is ever good. And the black Cadillac SUV with bulletproof windows parked beside it can only belong to one person.

Pushing up to my feet, I don't even bother brushing off my bloody knees or elbows. Instead, I storm up the steps to the two glass front doors and shove them open. "Dad?" It bounces off the high ceilings and grand foyer. I can't tell if my heart is pounding due to my fall or the fact that he's here.

What the hell?

"Dad!" I shout this time, storming down the long hallway and then running up the spiral staircase to his office

24

on the second floor. I come to the closed door and don't even bother knocking. Instead, I barge through it, sucking in breath after breath.

My gray sports bra is soaked in sweat, and my white capri yoga pants stick to my ass and legs as a result of my three-mile run. I don't give a shit that I don't look presentable and stink.

"Haven," my father announces to the room, jumping up from his seat behind his desk. Clearing his throat, he looks me up and down, the disapproval clear in his blue eyes.

"What is going on?" I demand, not even bothering with introductions.

My eyes slide to the man who slowly stands to my right. He towers over me at every bit of six feet four. His jet-black hair is parted on the right and combed over. His impressive charcoal suit with black button-down matches his shiny shoes. I know it costs him more than most hardworking men make in a year.

He looks the same as I remember him. *Intimidating.* Eyes so dark, they look like two endless black holes. He has his arms crossed over his chest, and the gold ring on his right hand looks like it could be used as a weapon. Why is he here? He lives in New York and very rarely makes appearances in Las Vegas. Well, or so I thought.

My father clears his throat. "Come here, Haven."

I search the room for the set of eyes that haunt me every time I close mine, but I don't see him.

"What's going on?" I ask again, standing my ground.

"You've been sold."

I spin around to face the man who spoke. He leans up against the wall next to the door I had just barged through. He's got a pair of dark jeans on and a white fitted shirt. A cigarette sits tucked behind his ear and his tatted arms are crossed over his chest. His matching black eyes fall to my sweat-covered yoga pants. Matteo was never as funny as he thought he was.

I narrow my eyes on him, and he runs his tongue over his upper lip. Turning back to my father, I ignore his ass, knowing that he just wants to wind me up. "What's really going on?"

He glares at Luca's younger brother, then looks back at me, but he says nothing. My heart skips a beat when his hard features soften, and he lets out a sigh, regret flashing across his face.

"Daddy ..." I walk over to his desk and place my sweaty hands on the cool surface. "What is going on?" I ask for a third time.

Looking down, I go to pick up the papers that sit on top of the dark wood, but he beats me to it and snatches them up.

"Are you deaf?" Matteo barks out. "I already told you. You've been sold."

I turn once again to face him as he pushes off the wall. "Bullshit!" I snap. I don't believe him for a second. "I am not for sale, and my father would never do that."

Where the fuck is Luca?

The corners of his lips turn up, and he comes to a stop before me. "People will do a lot for money," he says simply.

My stomach drops, but I shake my head. *Sold?* It's not even an option. The thought is unfathomable and, not to mention, illegal. "No," I whisper.

"Yes," he replies, lifting his right hand to touch my bare stomach. "We're here to collect. You'll marry ..."

"I won't marry you!" I interrupt, shoving him away.

Is he insane?

Matteo was a sick son of a bitch growing up. The

rumors about him at school would get a kid with lesser wealth thrown in prison for life, but the girls he chose to use never would step forward, and I hated it. The way he watched them walk by in the halls. The way he'd touch them without their permission, and they would physically shrink into themselves.

"You're right. You won't." His eyes skim over my heaving chest, naked torso, and yoga pants-clad thighs. "But you will be a Bianchi, nonetheless." He leans in closer, his lips nearly touching mine, and I have to swallow the bile that wants to rise at his closeness. He reeks of cigarettes and whores. The cheap kind. "And the Bianchis share everything they have."

Is he talking about his brother?

I almost laugh. Luca didn't want me then, and he won't want me now. Not as his wife. If he was here, lying in my bed naked and hard, then his car being outside would maybe make sense. But this doesn't.

I whip around to face my father once again, my loose hair slapping me in the face. "What the fuck is going on?" I shout, close to hysterics.

His face hardens. "Young lady, watch your language."

I ignore him. "Tell me this is some kind of joke. Why are they really here?" I snap.

I know my father has done business with them in the past. But for Luca's car to be out front is ... unsettling, to say the least. He's been gone for what feels like forever. Up and left me alone. He wouldn't come back now. Not for me.

My father won't look me in the eyes. He stares down at the papers in his hands, holding them out of my view. My heart pounds in my chest, and my voice breaks. "Daddy ..."

"Haven."

My chest tightens at the softness in his tone, and tears

sting my eyes. "I won't," I say even though I'm sure that Matteo is lying. This has to be a mistake. A misunderstanding.

He slaps the edge of his desk with the papers. My father is a tall guy at six foot three. I'm only five foot four. But then again, I'm not his biological child. His dark blue eyes glare down at me, and I shrink back. "It's done," he growls. "I don't wanna hear one more word from you!"

What's done? I wonder, shaking my head, but I can't make myself ask the words. A part of me knows, but I just don't understand why. My father would never do this. I've gotten in trouble in the past with the police—had a couple of rowdy years—and I know I still live at home at twenty-four, but I'm not that big of a problem. He wouldn't do this to get rid of me. Would he? "No."

Marriage?

To Luca Bianchi?

Why now? Why him?

I look at his father. "He won't agree to this."

He looks me up and down the same way Matteo did and gives me a smile that would scare any grown man. "It was his idea."

I take a step back from the desk, then another. I turn, yank open the door, and run out of his office. I stomp down the staircase, through the house, and out the back door. Tears run down my face, but I don't stop as I run across the stone path. Then my shoes hit the patch of synthetic grass that my mother had my father put in years ago. I round the in-ground pool and come to the rock wall. I reach up, gripping a hold and place my shoes in an open slot. Looking up, I begin to climb, but I scream out, letting go and falling to my ass. Adding another bruise to my already black and blue body. I scramble back as the man I've tried so hard to forget jumps down from where he was perched at the top. He was sitting in my favorite spot, waiting on me.

"Get back!" I shout.

Luca Bianchi stands before me with his hands tucked in his jeans. It's May, and he has a black leather jacket on over his white T-shirt but has left it unzipped. He always wears it. Some would think it's because he's cold natured, but I know it's to hide the gun and holster he wears. Last time I saw him was almost two years ago in this very spot. He lied to me, and then he left me. No text. No letter. Nothing. It was a common occurrence.

For too long I've been playing this cat and mouse game.

He no longer looks like the boy I once fell in love with. He was always on the skinny side back then, but he's filled out in all the right places. From what I can see, his arms are bigger, and he no longer shaves his face. He keeps it trimmed short, giving him a five o'clock shadow. And I hate how much I like it. How much it makes him look like a man.

His dark eyes rake over my bruised knees, my earlier fall leaving a hole in my yoga pants. Now the white spandex material is covered in blood along with dirt. Then they trail up my naked stomach and to my sports bra, and my nipples harden when he licks his luscious lips.

I cross my arms over my chest to try to cover them.

He grips his jeans-clad thighs, pulling the material up to allow him to kneel before me. "Hello, Haven."

Dread washes over me. Like a wave shoving me under the water, holding me hostage. "Why are you here, Luca? And don't give me any bullshit."

He tilts his head to the side, his eyes never leaving mine, and it makes me nervous. As if he's searching for something. I was always an open book when it came to him. Not only could he read my thoughts, but he would use my body. I would spread my legs for him like an avid reader would turn the pages of a book.

My heart pounds, and my breathing increases. I think I'm going to hyperventilate. Pass out.

"What do you mean by bullshit?" he asks.

He still takes me as a naïve woman who will believe everything he says. I've changed just as much on the inside as he has on the outside. My eyes narrow on him. "Cut the shit."

He sighs. "I'm here to give you what you've always wanted."

I eye him skeptically. The Bianchi men aren't fucking genies. They don't grant anyone a wish they want, unless it's something they know that can benefit them. "What I've always wanted?"

He reaches into the pocket of his leather jacket. My mouth goes dry at the sight of a black velvet box. "Luca ..."

"Me."

The single word has tears stinging my eyes, and my chest tightens. I wanted this for so long. For him to love me and want me. But it's a lie, and I won't live a life based on a lie. Not with him. Not for anyone.

"This is your favorite place." He gestures to the rock wall. I used to love to climb it before jumping into the pool. "This is where I first kissed you. Where I first told you I loved you." I flinch at those words. Just more lies. "Where I first fucked you ..."

"I get it!" I snap, pushing to my feet, and take a step back from him. He rises too and grips the box in his hand. My face tells him all he needs to know, and he is not pleased.

"I won't marry you." I shake my head, forcing my lips to

say the words out loud no matter how much it hurts my heart. He's all I've ever wanted.

"This isn't up for debate," he growls.

My head is spinning. I can't understand why he is here. Why he all of a sudden wants me. And to be his wife of all things. "Luca …"

"Do you know what I had to do to make this happen?"

My fear quickly turns to anger. *What he had to do?* "Don't try to make this sound like you want me," I snap. "This is only to benefit you in some way."

"Haven …"

"Or you would have married me two years ago." Tears sting my eyes.

"That was a long time ago," he says through gritted teeth.

"It still happened." I throw my arms out wide. "Right here in this very spot."

"Yes, and I regret it," he snaps.

My chest tightens at his words, and the first tear falls. His narrowed eyes soften, and he runs a hand through his dark hair, the action opening his leather jacket and showing me the black grip of his gun. My eyes go to his when he releases a sigh.

"I didn't mean that."

I swallow around the massive lump in my throat and try to control my breathing and calm my racing heart. I don't want to show him how much his words hurt me. I gave up on us a long time ago. But every time I finally felt ready to move on, he'd re-enter my life, and I'd fall back into his trap like the weak woman I am.

I hate it.

I hate myself.

"No, for once, you said exactly how you feel." I sniff,

running my hands down my face to erase the tears, and then I square my shoulders. "You don't have to pretend you want to be with me. Don't do me any favors." I turn, giving him my back, and return to the house. He follows me, but he remains silent.

Entering the back door, I make sure to slam it shut in his face. I hear him let out a curse before it's ripped open. I don't stop. Instead, I pick up my pace until I'm running down the hallway to the front of the house and take a right. I pass the guest bathroom and game room before I enter my room and gasp.

My entire Louis Vuitton luggage set sits on the floor at the foot of my bed along with my purse and backpack. "What the …?" I spin around to see Luca leaning against my doorframe with his arms crossed over his chest and eyes on mine. He watches me with a look of annoyance. Like he has somewhere to be, and I'm keeping him against his will. That tightness returns to my chest, and I shake my head as those damn tears begin to sting my eyes once again. "No." That's all I can say.

He pushes off the doorframe and walks over to me. I want to back away, but I'm frozen where I stand. Cupping my tear-streaked cheek, he whispers, "You belong to me now, Haven. And it's time to go home."

LUCA

Two years ago

I SIT ON *the rock wall, waiting for her to meet me. She told me she'd be here at eight, and it's now almost nine. I pull the leather jacket tighter around my chest, trying to block out the cold. For some godforsaken reason, it started snowing in*

Las Vegas twenty minutes ago. And the fact that the sun has set doesn't help.

Where the fuck is she?

At first, I was worried. I blew up her phone with calls and messages, but she ignored them all.

My teeth grind, and my fists clench. I'm Luca Bianchi, and I don't wait for any woman.

Making up my mind, I jump down from the wall. Just as I take my first step, I see her brown hair blowing in the wind. She has the white ski jacket on that I bought her last year for Christmas before I went with her and her family on their trip to the Alps.

I shove my hands in the pockets of my leather jacket and start walking over to her. "Where the fuck have you been?" *I demand.*

She has her head down, staring at the ground. The snow falls on her hair but melts instantly.

"Haven?" *I snap, coming up to her.* "I've been out here freezing my ass off." *Gripping her chin, I force her to look up at me, and her light brown tear-filled eyes meet mine.*

"I'm sorry." *Her perfectly white teeth chatter.*

"Hey." *I open my jacket and pull her body flush with mine immediately.* "What happened?" *I rub my hands along her back, trying to warm her up. Her body trembles against mine.* "Did something happen at school?" *I wonder.*

She's a senior this year in college. And that thought terrifies me. We haven't discussed what she will do after graduation. I've never had a choice. The family business is what I live for. It's what I was made for. But her? She could do anything. Go anywhere. The thought of her moving on and walking away from me is paralyzing, but inevitable. Especially since I have no choice but to leave her.

She shakes her head and grips my shirt. "I just need you."

My chest swells at her words. I love how much she loves me, how much she needs me, but I know she's lying. "Tell me. What's wrong? I'll take care of it."

I know her father does work with mine. He's in with the Mafia, and it scares the shit out of me. I've seen what they can do. Hell, I've done it. I wish I could shield her from what I know waits around the corner because she doesn't deserve this life. The bloody bodies and blackmail. Maybe her leaving Nevada could be the best thing for her. Maybe me leaving her is the best thing for her.

She pulls back, her dark eyes look up into mine, and a single tear runs down her face. "I love you," she whispers brokenly.

Reaching up, I cup her cold cheek. "I love you, Haven."

"Run away with me."

"What?"

She pulls away from my arms, and I allow it, too stunned by her words. "Run away with me." She takes my hands, and a smile graces her gorgeous face. "Please, Luca? I know where my father has a lot of money stashed. I can get it, and we can run away. We can change our names and move to an island where no one will ever find us. Just you and me." She releases me and places her hands flat on my chest.

I remove them and take a step back from her. Her face falls and so does my stomach as I say, "I can't."

"You have to. I overheard ..." She stops herself. Her eyes widen for the briefest second, and she licks her lips, wrapping her arms around herself.

My jaw tightens. "What did you hear?"

She bites her bottom lip nervously.

"Haven?" I snap, gripping her shoulders. "What did you hear?"

She sniffs. "Your dad was here. And I overheard him telling mine that he's sending you on a job."

Fuck!

"You're going to Italy," she cries, breaking her silence. "He's sending you away, Luca. He's going to make you ..." She trails off, staring up at me. Her face morphs from panic, to pain, and then to anger. "You know," she whispers. "What ... when ...?" She shakes her head.

I run a hand down my face. "I ..."

"Were you going to tell me?" she shouts, shoving my chest.

I didn't want her to find out this way. "Haven ..."

"He's going to get you killed!" she screams, her fists hitting my chest. "Don't you see that? You're not like them, Luca."

But I am. She doesn't know about half the shit I've done or the people I've killed. When she's around, I always hide the dark and evil side that comes so naturally to me. She makes me think that I can be better. That maybe, just maybe, I don't have to be a monster.

"Please." She grips my jacket. "Please don't go."

"Haven ..."

"Pick me," she cries, and my chest tightens. If only it were that easy. "Please, run away with me. I'll give up everything for you, Luca. I'm asking you to do the same." She drops to her knees as if her legs can no longer hold her up.

I drop to mine as well and pull her small body onto my lap. I close my eyes and hold her. They pop open the moment she shifts to straddle me. Her freezing hands go to either side of my face, but I don't even flinch. The desperation in her eyes chills me to the bone. "I love you. We can do this. I know *we can. We deserve this chance, Luca. To be free and live our lives together. Like we've discussed so many times."*

I've thought that a million times.

"If not for you, do it for me. I need you." She licks her chattering lips. "Please don't leave me. Run away and marry me."

I cup her face and let out a long breath, knowing I have a choice to make. And I know it's the right one. "I meant it when I told you I loved you, Haven. More than anything in this world." Her eyes light up with newfound hope. "And, of course. I'll do it for you. For us."

Present

I LIED TO her.

It's easy to feed someone lies when you know they're starving.

Right then and there, I told her I'd be back the following day to get her. That I had some contacts I could call, and that we needed twenty-four hours to get our stuff together to get out of the country. In order to spend the rest of our lives together, we'd need to spend the night apart.

Three hours later, I boarded a private jet with a heavy heart. It was the best thing to do at the time. We wouldn't have been able to run and live the life I wanted us to have. I was called to serve, and no one runs from the Mafia. Not even Luca Bianchi. They would have skinned me alive for my betrayal. It would have been painful. I've seen it done, and I would have ended up in a shallow grave after a week of enduring the torture.

But Haven? My father might have taken her in as his own personal whore. Or sold her off to his best friend. Or even worse, handed her over to my brothers. I couldn't have done that to her. So I lied. I hurt her, knowing I'd have to win her back when I returned. Things aren't the same since I left for Italy. I'm no longer a boy trying to fight the inevitable. I'm a Bianchi, and the Bianchis live and die by the code.

Standing here in her bedroom, watching her stare at me with hatred and fear won't deter my plans. I knew this day would come. Even if I had to rip up the floor underneath her feet and carry her out kicking and screaming, she would be mine.

TWO

HAVEN

E REACHES FOR my hand. I go to pull it away, but he's faster. He yanks me out of my room and up the stairs. I feel my chest tighten as we walk down the hallway. I know where we're going, and I dig my running shoes into the floor to try to stop us.

It doesn't work.

Coming up to the door I barged through earlier, he places his large hand firmly on the small of my bare back. Opening the door, he pushes me in. I come to a quick stop as three sets of eyes look at me.

"There's the bride-to-be." His father smiles at me.

My stomach drops at his words. Like an anchor out in a bottomless ocean, pulling me deeper and deeper into the dark water, unable to get a breath. The light from the sky above gets dimmer with every second.

"Haven," my father says my name.

My watery eyes go to his, and he doesn't look the least bit sorry. Or worried. "Why?" I croak out. My family knows how much Luca leaving destroyed me. My mother tried to distract me with expensive things, but my father just avoided it completely.

He tilts his head to the side, looking at me with concern as if I'm about to have a nervous breakdown. I think the situation warrants it. I wonder if he would place me in a mental facility if I refuse to do this? Can a father do that to a daughter when she's legally an adult? I'm sure he could. But a straitjacket and a padded room would be better than being a Bianchi. Better than serving out a life sentence with a man I hate because he made me a fool.

"I already told you. Money."

I turn to see Matteo is still leaning up against the wall by the door. His black eyes, that match his father's, drop to my chest again and then my stomach. I wrap my arms around myself, hating how exposed I am. I should have changed while I was in my room.

A firm hand grabs my upper arm, spinning me around. I look up to see Luca glaring down at me. He shrugs out of his leather jacket and places it over my shoulders. I quickly shove my arms into the warm sleeves, thankful for the cover even if it does swallow me. My eyes fall to the gun holster that rests on his shoulders and the black .380 that sits in its place. I'm not afraid of guns because I was raised around them. My father is always carrying and so is my mother. Plus, being so close to the Bianchis, they always had bodyguards around who were armed.

I have the thought of taking it from him to shoot his father with it, but where would that get me? Luca doesn't love me. He has proven time and time again that his loyalty does not lie with me. And as much as I hate him right now, I don't want to die.

"Let's get down to business, shall we?" My father claps his hands, and I jump at the sound.

"Yes, I must be getting back to New York," Luca's father agrees. As much business as John Bianchi does here, he hates being in Vegas. He has men here, like Luca, who take care of his shit for him. Luca runs the show, and Matteo plays a close second. "The party to announce the engagement will be this Friday. At Luca's."

That's in two days.

"And the wedding will be in two weeks," he adds. "It will be held at St. Mary's Cathedral, and the reception will be here."

"No one will believe it," I whisper, my throat tightening.

"Oh, they will." His father nods once. "Because if not, there will be consequences."

My knees threaten to buckle at his threat. It was delivered so calmly, sweetly even, but I know he's serious. The man is known for slaughtering people. His family has always been in the media. He's been arrested for murders but never convicted. He either pays them off or keeps his hands clean. Either way, he's not to be fucked with.

Luca ushers me over to a black leather chair in front of my father's desk.

"I will admit, this is unusual. Most mafioso weddings, the bride is always a virgin." John gives me a sly grin. "But we are all fully aware that my son popped that cherry years ago."

I think I'm gonna be sick.

My father opens a drawer, and my heart pounds when I see him remove the paperwork from earlier and place it down on the surface.

"No." I jump to my feet. "I won't do this."

"Haven—" Luca begins.

His father interrupts him, spitting out some Italian I

41

don't understand. Four years of two different foreign languages and I never took Italian. Luca and I always joked that he would teach me, but we never got around to it.

Luca snaps something back, and his father squares his shoulders. Then his eyes land on mine. I take a step back.

"I've already signed it," my father growls. "And so have the Bianchis."

A vise grips my chest, and I shake my head. He rounds the desk, picking up the papers, and when I go to turn around and leave, he grabs my hand, squeezing my fingers together.

"Ow, Daddy," I cry out. "You're hurting me."

He yanks me to the desk, and I stumble over my own feet, falling into it. He grips the back of my neck and holds me over it. My palms hit the surface, and I'm gasping for a breath. The tears pricking my eyes keep me from being able to read the words on the white paper before me. "Sign it!" my father yells.

I shake my head. The tears that were clouding my vision fly, but new ones instantly replace them. "I won't ..."

He places a pen in my left hand and then wraps his hand around mine, crushing my fingers together painfully. I yank it away, and his large wedding ring cuts my finger. I stumble back, holding my hand to my chest.

My father straightens, and his blue eyes look at me with disappointment. I've never seen him like this. He's never treated me remotely close to this. Why now? Why them?

"Fine," he growls, then leans over the table and signs my name for me.

"That'll never hold up in court," I spit at him, my chest constricting from his betrayal.

"We are the court," Luca's father says with a sinister smile.

I fist my hands, my nails digging into my skin. Angry and fucking broken, I stand here helpless. What did I do for him to give me away so easily? Had he planned this all along?

I look over at Luca, and he's glaring at my father's smug smile. He doesn't want me. This is his father's doing. He left me and didn't plan on coming back. But our fathers got together and devised this insane plan to connect our families together. The only question is why? We're not Mafia. My father isn't a mob boss. That I know of.

"Nite." Luca calls out a name, and I jump back when a man steps out from the shadowy corner.

Oliver Nite. They call him Silent Nite. He doesn't speak, not anymore, and I don't know why he took a vow of silence. How long has he been there? He looks at Luca, his large, muscular arms down by his sides. He'd be really attractive if not for his angry expression and kill-all attitude.

"Remove Haven from the room," he orders.

I have a moment of panic when my throat closes on me. I don't want to be in here, but I also don't want to be with Nite either. We were never close. He's a Bianchi. A killer.

When I go to protest, Luca's eyes land on mine, and there's a challenge in them. To defy him. To force his hand. To give him a chance to prove to the other men in this room that he fucking owns me. My mother taught me to pick my battles, and as I stand in a room with five very powerful men, I know the battles haven't even begun yet.

LUCA

THE DOOR SHUTS as Nite removes Haven from the room.

I whirl on her dad, my hand wrapping around his

throat. I practically throw him down onto his desk. "Luca …"

I squeeze, taking away his air, and lean over him. "Don't ever fucking touch her again. Do you understand?"

His blue eyes narrow up at me. His hands gripping my wrist that holds him captive.

"Do you understand?" Reaching over with my free hand, I pick up the pen he used to sign her name and stab him in the arm with it and release his neck.

"You son of a bitch …" He growls as he rolls off the side of the desk. Coughing, he rights himself and yanks the pen free from his upper arm, throwing it onto the desk. It wasn't much, but it'll be a reminder. "You little shit!"

I fist my right hand and swing, the hit knocking him into the bookshelf behind his desk. His eyes roll into the back of his head, and he goes limp long enough to fall to the floor. He comes to seconds later, and I grip his suit jacket, hauling his ass to his feet. Getting in his face, I growl, "You handed her over. She no longer belongs to you and no longer answers to you. She is now mine. I will do with her as I see fit, and I will punish her how I see fit. Do you understand me?" I'm shouting. I can feel my pulse jumping in my neck. My body physically shakes with my anger.

I wanted to rip his fucking hand off when she cried out that he was hurting her. But I had to show some restraint in front of her. My father's present, and this is just another test. I won't treat Haven the way he treats my mother. I will stand up for my wife. But I will make sure every mother-fucker knows I control her. I own her.

"Yes," he finally growls, and I shove him backward.

I ignore my father's smug smile and my brother's cocked eyebrow and storm out of the office.

THREE
HAVEN

T wo years ago

I LIE IN MY BED, CURLED UP IN A BALL. I HAVEN'T moved in hours. I don't know the time, but the sun has set.

I've done nothing but cry. I can't eat, can't sleep. My heart hurts too much.

Luca left me. He told me he loved me, and that we would run away together, and then he just ... poof ... was gone. I've been calling him, but it goes straight to voicemail. My texts go unanswered. I keep telling myself I need to move on and come to terms with it, but I can't. I refuse to believe that all this time has been a lie.

"Haven?" my mother whispers my name, entering my room. "Honey, you need to eat something."

"Not hungry." My voice is hoarse from all the sobbing.

The bed dips behind me, and I feel her hand on my back. "What can I get you to eat? You'll feel better if—"

"He never loved me," I interrupt her and squeeze my eyes closed.

"I don't believe that, and neither do you."

I turn over and look up at her. "Then why would he leave me?"

She sighs, running her hand over my shoulder. "Some things can't be explained, Haven. The world that Luca lives in is different than most. Maybe, in a way, he thought he was doing what was best for you."

"No," I cry. "Him leaving isn't what's best for me."

"Come here." She opens her arms wide, and I get up and crawl into them.

Hugging her tightly, I cry on her shoulder. I don't know what hurts more. The fact that he so easily said goodbye, or the fact that I can't help but still love him.

PRESENT

FROM WHERE I'M SITTING IN THE PASSENGER SEAT OF Luca's car, I look over to see him exit the front door to my parents' house. He jogs down the stone steps. Once he reaches the bottom, he stops and speaks to Nite, who only nods a few times at whatever Luca is saying before he walks toward the car.

I quickly wipe the tears from my face, not wanting him to see me like this. So broken. So defeated. I just signed a contract. Well, my father signed it for me, but Luca's father was right. They are the court. They own this city. They don't call it Sin City for nothing. The worst part is, I have no idea what was on that contract. And that terrifies me.

He gets into the car, slamming the door shut, and peels out, causing the tires to squeal on the driveway.

I sit in the passenger seat of his limited-edition car. He cherishes it. I wish I had eaten breakfast so I could throw up right here and now, but my stomach is empty. My heart shattered.

It's time to go home.

I've dreamed of him telling me that before, but it wasn't because he bought me. It was because he couldn't live without me. My parents threw me to the wolves, knowing he could rip me to shreds.

How long has he been sitting on this? How long has he known he was going to show up at my father's house today and have my mother pack my things and remove me from the house?

A while.

Luca never does anything without thinking it through first. He's been trained to think of every possible outcome. Every option. He was designed to get the most out of every situation. A part of me knows I can't blame him. It's not his fault his father is a Don. And he is to follow in his footsteps.

We remain silent in the car, except for his radio. "Devil's in the Backseat" by Lostboycrow plays, and with every second that passes, my heart grows more heavy.

He comes to a stop, pressing a button on his dash, and the black wrought-iron gate pushes open. We pull forward, and I see the mansion he calls home before us.

It's everything I ever wanted and everything that I despise at the same time. He drives underneath the breezeway that connects the house to the five-car detached garage, then pulls around the circular driveway in the back. A pool sits off to the left in front of a pool house.

He gets out and walks around to open my door, but I

jump out before he can get to it. No need to pretend to be a gentleman.

He reaches for my hand. I go to yank it away, but he's faster. His grip tightens, and I flinch. He pulls me under the back porch, and I look over the lawn furniture that takes up the large space. It's a cream color with burnt orange throw pillows. A hammock sits over in the corner tied off to two big palm trees. It has a state-of-the-art full-size kitchen with a brick fireplace. Only the best when it comes to a Bianchi.

He shoves the glass door open, and we enter the house. I take a quick look around. I've been here a thousand times. His father bought him this place after he graduated high school, which was convenient for us. It's not like we had to hide our relationship before. His father didn't care, and my mother turned a blind eye to my sex life. She liked to think it didn't exist, and my father never seemed to disapprove. Now I'm wondering if this is why. Did he and Luca's dad have this planned all along?

I would stay over, and when I'd wake, he would already be gone for the day. I would pretend I was his wife and run around the house in his T-shirt. It was a dream I desperately wanted to come true.

Careful what you wish for. Your dream can quickly become your worst nightmare.

He opens his bedroom door, and the moment he releases my hand, I come to a stop.

"Your things will be delivered soon." His words are flat, but they cut me like a knife. He's so cold. And I can feel his anger. "You have your own closet ..."

"I'm not putting my things in here." I finally find my voice.

He turns to face me. "Yes. You are."

I shake my head. "I refuse ..."

"Will you stop?" he snaps, making me flinch at the sharpness of his tone. He's never spoken to me like this in the past. What did he do in Italy that changed him so much? "Stop acting like this scared little kitten, Haven." He storms back over to me. "This is not a death sentence. This is our home now."

I snort, finding that fire as well. "You think I'm gonna lie down and sleep with you in a bed you've fucked your whores in?" I ask tightly.

I hate the fact that I haven't been with a single man since he left me. Now I wish I would have fucked anyone who looked my way. I know he has.

He leans in, his lips softly grazing my ear. His scent that I used to want to cover myself in now smells sour. "It's never stopped you before."

I fist my hands and shove him away from me. He doesn't budge. Instead, his hands grip my head, and he tilts it back. His lips devour mine a second later. His kiss is like pain—it demands to be felt. So fucking much that it makes me weak in the knees.

He tastes like everything I hate and love all at once. His tongue enters my mouth, and I try to pull away, but he nips at my lip, and I whimper. I kiss him back. Aggressively. I take all my hate and pour it into this kiss. Hoping he chokes on it.

I bite his lip hard, and his hands slides into my hair, fisting it. My scalp feels like a thousand pinpricks. He bites down on my lip this time, and I taste blood.

He pulls back, and I suck in a breath, trying to clear my thoughts. My mind. This is his plan. This is how he will cage me in a luxurious mansion and make me never want to leave. And I'm not sure I'll be able to fight it.

His dark eyes roam my face. He lifts his hand, and I

flinch. His face grows hard as stone. "Have I ever hit you?" he questions with a growl.

"No," I answer softly.

"I'm not going to beat you, Haven." He releases a sigh and leans his head forward, resting his forehead on mine.

I hold my breath.

"But I need you to understand that when I tell you that you will be my wife." He pulls back and hard eyes stare down at me. "I will be your husband. And we will share this bed."

Then he steps back and exits the room, closing the door behind him.

LUCA

I SIT IN my Bugatti La Voiture Noire in the middle of the night. The lights are off and so is the radio. Thankfully, the row of bushes I'm hiding behind is low enough to the ground to cover us while still giving me a clear view of the wedding chapel across the street. Twenty years ago, it was a funeral home, but then Alberto Rossi turned it into a wedding chapel. Guess he felt the living would bring him more money than the dead. And he just needed a cover.

My brother sits in the passenger seat, driving me nuts by blowing bubbles with his gum. "If you pop one more bubble, I'm gonna stab you in the neck with my knife." I finally speak to him.

He snorts. "Someone isn't getting enough pussy. What's wrong? The soon-to-be Mrs. Bianchi not spreading her legs for you?"

I ignore him. My sex life is none of his business. No matter how right he may be.

I left Haven standing in our room earlier today and

haven't seen her since. I had work to do. Honestly, I'm pretty pissed at her. I thought she'd be happy. She's always wanted marriage, a home, and children, and I'm going to give her that. I think she was more upset that she had been sold than the fact she had to marry me. I wasn't going to tell her that I bought her. I had planned to keep that a secret, but my brother fucking ruined it. Just like he does everything.

"Just a tip, I wouldn't eat whatever she cooks you. Poison isn't that hard to come by."

Headlights shine ahead of us, and a limo pulls up in the roundabout. A guy dressed in a pair of holey jeans and a wrinkled T-shirt climbs out of the back. He helps a very drunk looking redhead out behind him. They enter the chapel hand in hand.

"I'm not sure what you expected," he continues. "You left her. She'll always hate you for that."

"I had no choice."

He snorts. "She may believe your bullshit, but we both know you had a choice." He looks over at me. "You chose the wrong girl."

My hands fist the steering wheel. "What's done is done." I made a decision, and I've lived with it for almost two years now. She'll either get over it, or she won't. At this point, it doesn't really matter. The world will know she's my wife.

He nods at that. "Dad is—"

"I don't care to talk about Dad and what he is," I interrupt him. He doesn't want me with Haven. He had other plans for me, but I won't allow him to dictate my life. He has three other sons he can do that to.

I cross my arms over my chest, and the couple comes rushing out the glass door. She carries a black bouquet in her right hand. He picks her up, throwing her over his shoulder, and he slaps her ass before he places her back in the limo, and it takes off.

My brother sighs. "We've been here for over two hours. Maybe you got it wrong."

"I didn't," I growl.

"What exactly did Titan tell you?"

I lean my head back against the headrest. I've told him this a hundred times now. "The Queen said she heard the client on his phone. He said there would be a drop tonight. No time. But she was positive Rossi was mentioned."

"Sure, she was." He snorts. Silence falls over the car once again, but it only lasts a few seconds before he speaks. "What do you think Rossi is up to? Why hasn't he come after us?"

I've asked myself this very question every day for the past four years. Nite and I took six of his men on the mountain that day. Why not make his move? The mob isn't known for their patience. If they want you dead, they will pull up to your house, your kids' school, or even your church and shoot you right between your eyes and then drive away.

"What if this is a setup?" He goes on. "They could have paid the hooker a hefty amount in return for her to make up this fake drop. We run in. They kill us. Boom. All a lie."

I run a hand down my face. "Guess we'll just have to wait and see." I see headlights coming toward us, and a white utility van follows shortly behind it. "We won't have to wait long." I reach over and hit him in the shoulder.

He sits up straighter, picks up the gun in his lap, and loads the magazine into his .380. All jokes aside for now.

I do the same and look over at him. "Stay with me."

He nods.

"I mean it," I growl. Last time we did a *job*, he skipped

out on me and ended up getting shot in the arm. You would have thought the fucker was dying. I even had to carry him.

"I know—"

"No, you don't," I interrupt him. "Stay the fuck with me, or I'll shoot you myself."

"Yeah, yeah." He shoves open the passenger door and jumps out.

I exit as well, and he follows me across the dark street over to the chapel. Running, I come to the side and push my back up against the brick building. I hold the gun in front of me and aim, ready to shoot at any given second.

"Is this all of it?" a man asks. I recognize the voice. It's Rossi's right-hand man, Donatello. He replaced Bernard, the guy I left for dead on the side of the mountain four years ago.

Rossi and my father once were friends, and they worked together until they went their separate ways. Nobody knows what happened except for them. Honestly, I'm surprised they're both still alive. For the most part, we stay on our side of Vegas, and he stays on his. Then he came after my family, and all bets were off.

But once again, tonight, we're going to him. We're going to take from him again. Because I don't care what I have to do once I enter those back doors, but every one of his men that I see tonight will be dying. I'm going to tip the scales in the Bianchi favor. And my marriage to my college sweetheart is going to push my family to the front of that war. It doesn't matter if she's always loved me, or if she now hates me. It's business. My life has always been that way, and I'm not about to change now. Not when my family needs me, plus it gets me what I want. *Her*.

"No. There's one more bag in the truck," an unfamiliar voice answers him.

"Go and get it," Donatello demands. "It's late, and I wanna get the fuck home."

"Yes, sir."

I walk down the side of the brick building until I come to the back. I peek my head around the corner to see a man dressed in dark jeans and a black T-shirt walk over to the white van. The double doors in the back are open. He leans over and grabs a trash bag.

I shove my gun in the waistband of my jeans, remove my knife from my black boot, and rush over to him. I come up from behind, slap my hand over his mouth, and yank his head back. Then I slash his neck from ear to ear, making sure to dig the knife in deep enough to get the job done.

Blood sprays across the bag and on the back of the van. His body goes limp, and I remove my hand from his mouth. He falls to his knees, then forward, his head hitting the back bumper before he slumps to the ground and bleeds out.

I step back and run the side of the blade across my black jeans before placing it back in my boot. Grabbing the bag, I throw it at my younger brother. "Take this back to the car."

He arches a brow. "What about ...?"

"Now, Matteo," I snap, knowing I told him earlier to stay next to me at all times. I'm not in the mood to listen to his shit right now. I have blue balls and need to get this over with.

He lets out a sigh but turns and runs back to my car to put the bag away.

One down.

Picking up the dead body, I throw his fat ass into the back of the van and shut the doors. Not much I can do about the blood on the ground, but the cleanup crew will take care of that once I make the call.

Pulling my gun back out, I open the back door of the

building and creep inside the chapel. It's quiet, letting me know that whatever is happening is upstairs. Rossi never transformed it like the first floor.

I make my way up the stairs quietly, my gun steady in my hands. Once I hit the landing, I look both left and right. It's cold. Doesn't matter how long the funeral home has been out of use, the smell of dead bodies lingers. It's in the walls. No amount of bleach or paint could ever cover it up. That's why I'm so surprised anyone would want to get married below it.

I make my way down the long hallway, and a single light buzzes above my head. The old, flowered wallpaper ripped off in spots. The brown carpet stained and chunks missing. I come up to a door on my left and crack it open. It's empty other than the two large side-by-side metal plated crematories.

Hmm, we can make use of that.

Closing the door, I continue, opening the next one. The concrete floor is covered in dried blood, and the back wall has three metal doors. This is where they store the bodies. There are two metal slabs with sinks at the end where they wash them off before placing them inside the refrigeration system.

Entering the room, I shut the door behind me softly. Walking over to the doors, I open one up, but it's empty. I close it and open the next one. To my surprise, it has a body. I thought it was out of commission. But we've always suspected the chapel to be a front. A tag on his toe tells me his name was Jacob Miller. Thirty years old and was an organ donor.

I bet he was.

This is what they did in the past. They'd steal bodies from the hospital, remove all the organs, and then pack their

55

bodies full of drugs and or money. Then they ship them. Hard for search dogs to recognize the smell of drugs when you have a rotting corpse in front of them.

"He's in here," a voice calls out.

Shit!

Closing the door, I open the one that I know was empty and crawl in. I lie down and look up into total darkness. This would frighten any person, except for me. For my family. I saw my first dead body at ten years old when my father killed my uncle. At the time, I was scared of what he was capable of, but it didn't take me long to understand. A month after my uncle's murder, my aunt Ava was gunned down in her own home. My father didn't make me witness that one.

The Mafia takes their code of silence very seriously. You don't fucking talk. To anyone, about anything.

"When are they shipping out?" a familiar voice asks, and my jaw clenches. Davis Ricardo is Rossi's most loyal follower, but he wants to be number one. He wants to be the one on top and in charge, and in order to achieve that, he'll have to fuck him over. It's just a matter of time. He'll get tired of waiting. Eventually.

"Tomorrow. Don't want them sitting still for too long. We'll put them on the plane and fly them out. They'll reach their destination by Friday."

No, they won't.

"Okay, put the woman in this one." I hear him slap the door to the one I'm in.

Shit!

I hit the side of my Apple watch to light up what small amount of space I can see. Thankfully, it's open. Normally, these would have individual slots for each body, but these bastards can be cheap, and they chose to purchase the kind where each level is open, so it costs less to cool.

Thank God for that.

I quickly crawl over, trying to be quiet, and hold my gun so I don't drop it on the metal tables. The space is cramped and cold. Once I get to the next one that is available, I lie back down and close my eyes, turning off my light.

Where in the fuck is my brother?

"How long will it take?" Donatello asks.

"Shouldn't take me longer than thirty minutes to pack the body."

"Get it done," he orders.

I smile to myself, ready to get this show started. I can take them all on at once, but I prefer one at a time.

I hear the door open to the room. "Sir? Gabe is dead."

Fuck!

"What?" Donatello snaps.

"I found him in the back of the van," a man rushes out. "Throat slashed."

"Find whoever did this," he barks. "I want the place surrounded. Now!"

"Yes, sir."

Then the room grows silent. I hold my breath to listen for any kind of noise but hear nothing. I open the door and peek out, looking for my brother. Nothing.

"I want everything shipped tonight," Donatello orders from down the hall, but I can't see him. "Someone, some-where has fucking opened their mouth."

"But sir, the pickup van won't be here until tomorrow."

"Then make a fucking phone call and assure me that it will depart tonight," he barks. "If you don't make this happen, I will stuff your body with these fucking drugs myself."

Walking down the hall with my back pressed into a wall, I hold my gun up and turn the corner. I see Donatello standing at the end of another hall with two guys flanking each side. His bodyguards. He wears a black suit with a red button-up, and a black and white tie, cutting into his double chin. His once dark hair is now shaved close to his head. He holds a cigar in one hand and a gun in the other.

"I think we should evacuate, sir," one of them suggests.

He snorts. "Rossi will kill each one of us if we don't get this shit moved."

Ricardo comes into view. "I'll stay behind and take care of it. You need to leave. I'll call Rossi and inform him of what is happening," he says, running a hand down his stubble. He's nervous. Good.

Rossi will question his loyalty. Not because he'll think he talked, but because he'll think he got careless and somehow tipped someone off and was followed.

I raise my gun and aim it right at Donatello, waiting for Ricardo to move out of my way to give me a clear shot.

"Fine," he growls. "I'm going." Ricardo takes a step forward, giving me a clear shot, and I take it. But at the last minute, he moves again, and the bullet whizzes right past him. Ricardo leaps on top of him, shoving him to the tile floor. With guns raised, they aim them in my direction, and I jump out of the way, falling to my side and sliding across the floor as gunfire erupts in the small space. I pull the trigger, over and over until there's nothing left. Pieces of the wall and ceiling fall down around me. Jumping up, I run into an adjoining room, shutting the door behind me. I drop the now empty magazine and replace it with another one I pull from my pocket before aiming at the door. It opens, and I go to shoot but see that it's my brother.

I lower my gun. "Where the fuck have you been?" I whisper harshly.

He turns to face the door as well. His shirt is covered in blood along with his hands. He's wiping them on his pants. "Was on my way back from the car and saw two men walking out the front."

"And?" I snap at his vagueness.

"Killed Isaac. The other got away," he explains with a growl. My brother hates to lose.

We were raised to be competitive. He once played baseball for our high school. He was removed from the team after he slammed his fist into the coach's face when he was made to run a lap after striking out in practice. That was his one and only week as a Tiger.

"What about you? Killed any more?"

I shake my head and walk over to the door. "Nope. But we need to wrap this up."

He nods once.

I take a deep breath and kick open the door, a gun in both hands. Holding them out, I'm ready to shoot at anything, but we're met with silence. As I look around, my eyes narrow. What are they doing? Where did they go?

Tires squeal, and I run down the stairs to the back door, flinging it open. The taillights of the van are fading in the distance. I aim and fire off more rounds, but none of them make contact. "Fuck!"

My brother chuckles from behind me. "Man, has she fucked with your mind? It hasn't even been a full twenty-four hours yet. Since when do you miss?"

I spin around, pointing the gun at his head. "I bet I won't miss from here." I arch a brow.

He just smiles at me. "You're out of bullets."

"Am I?" I question. Lowering the gun, I pull the trigger, sending a bullet into the floor. Right between his feet.

He jumps back. "Fuck, man. What the fuck?"

"Don't fuck with me, Matteo. I'm not in the mood," I warn.

His eyes narrow on mine, but he says nothing. I release the magazine and pull my last one free of my holster. "Come on, I'm ready to get this shit over with."

I enter the room again with all the bodies to find a man standing with his back to us. He's shoving a pack of drugs into the dead body. I come up behind him and press the gun to the back of his head.

He whimpers and throws his hands up.

"I'll take this." My brother speaks, yanking the gun from his hip, and points it along with his own at him.

"Is this all of it?" I demand.

He says nothing.

"I'll give you one more chance to answer me."

"I'm not telling you shit." He spins around to face me.

And to my surprise, I know the guy. He's the son of my father's right-hand man. "Anthony." I smile. "What are the odds of running into you here?"

"Fuck you, Luca!" he screams in my face.

"I'll fuck your mouth." My brother wiggles his eyebrows. "It's all the same to me, baby."

Anthony's jaw sharpens, and he turns to jump my brother, but he slams the butt of the gun into his head, knocking him out. Anthony falls to the floor, and my brother and I both listen for any other noises.

"I think they left."

"They'll be back," I say.

Rossi thought he had a foolproof operation because no one has ever dared to attack on his territory. It made him vulnerable. Weak. He had less men than usual. We've never made such a bold move. My father has always been the one behind the operations, but tonight was my doing. I called the shots, and we needed to make ourselves very clear. My marriage to Haven is going to solidify that. Her father is going to make us untouchable. More than we already are.

"Get him up," I order.

"What are we doing with him?" he asks.

"I saw a crematory at the end of the hall." I nod to the door. "Let's go drop him in there and turn it on. We'll leave his ashes for them to find when they return."

FOUR
LUCA

I NOTICE THE clock on my dash shows a little after three a.m. We pull up to the back of Kingdom—the most prestigious hotel and casino here in Las Vegas. It gives them all a run for their money.

After getting out of the car, we walk up the fifteen stairs to the black double doors with a suitcase rolling behind me. I push one open while my brother chooses to use the revolving door. Entering the hotel, my shoes clap on the white marble floor. A big gold K sits in the middle of a black circle. The inside looks just as exquisite as the outside. A gold chandelier hangs from the high, mirrored ceiling. Black and gold accents are hung on the walls, and it smells like every person's dream. Money. Instant gratification. Most enter a hotel on the Strip to win big. To catch that high that only a casino can give them. Where days feel like hours and hope smells like cigarettes. But this is a private entrance. No one is allowed back here unless cleared. There are no slot machines. No blackjack tables.

"Luca." A man by the name of Nigel greets me, giving me a nod when he spots me from behind the black marble desk. "How is your morning going, sir?" His brown eyes look over my bloodstained jeans. I had an extra shirt in the car but didn't have a chance to change my pants. But he's not surprised. He sees all kinds of shit here. His bosses don't mind getting their hands dirty either.

"Rather good. Yours?" My brother snorts at my choice of words.

"Excellent, sir. Mine as well." He walks over to a private elevator that has the same black circle with the gold K in the middle. He scans a key card for access. The door slides open, and the three of us enter the mirrored box. The floor is black marble with gold specks that look like confetti.

He scans his key card yet again, and the doors close.

This elevator only stops on a few select floors. One of them is the thirteenth. Most buildings choose to leave this floor unused due to superstitions, but the Kings don't believe in bullshit such as old wives' tales. They do their most exclusive work on that floor.

The door slides open, and Nigel gestures for us to exit. "After you, sir."

We step off the elevator, walk through another set of double doors, and immediately enter the conference room. Four men sit at a custom black stone table that could easily fit twenty. It has a large skull carved out of the middle with Kingdom written in gold letters at each end. The thick black curtains are pulled closed, covering up the opposite wall of windows to hide us from the world even though it's the middle of the night. You can never be too careful.

My brother plops down in one of the black leather chairs and leans back in it, chewing away on a toothpick. I toss the suitcase onto the surface and sit down.

"Thank you, Nigel," Bones says from the head of the table, dismissing him.

"My pleasure, sir." He folds his arms behind his back and nods before backing out of the room, closing the black double doors behind him.

I pull my cell out of my front pocket and set it on the table in front of me, making sure it's in sight, even though I know the moment we stepped off the elevator the jammers took away any signal. These guys don't fuck around. That's why we do business with them.

The Dark Kings are known for many things—and tolerance is not one of them. You betray them; they kill your ass. No questions asked. Just like us.

I remember one time, as a child, sitting in church and the preacher discussing the satanic bible and the four satanic crown princes of hell; Lucifer, Leviathan, Satan and Belial.

Belial is the closest to Bones as I can see. See, in the satanic bible, Belial was associated with independence, the earth, and the north, the direction of darkness. He was also frequently associated with sex, lust, confusion, and darkness. All things that Bones lives for.

Leviathan, who I associate with Titan, is the great sea monster, sexual desire from the unknown and feared depths. He's an unstoppable force from within a man. And associated with water and west.

Lucifer would be Grave; bringer of light, enlightenment. He is a person's inner light that society attempts to drag into the darkness of conformity.

Then there's Satan. AKA Cross. The adversary of mundanity, mediocrity, right-hand path, stupidity. Self-destruction, religion, and Gods. He is associated with the element of fire and south. And his father was also the preacher. But believe me when I say, Cross was just like his father.

Our arrangement was solidified long before any of us were born. The Dark Kings didn't start the alliance. No, their fathers did—the Three Wisemen made a deal with my father back in the late eighties. That was also when the Three Wisemen started Kingdom. Now at twenty-six, their sons run it like a well-oiled machine. They were all raised like me and my brothers—were getting our hands dirty before we knew any different. So, we continued that alliance and struck a new deal. We cover the streets, and they cover the sheets. They have eyes and ears everywhere. They thrive off other people's addictions. Drugs, gambling, and alcohol to name just a few. And sex—it can be very powerful when used properly.

Titan sits next to me with his inked arms crossed over his chest. The guy thinks he's God's gift to women. Hence the nickname Titan. He rules over the queens—the ladies of the night—and is also head of security here at Kingdom.

Grave sits across from me. The guy has a death wish. Has since he was a kid. I'll never forget the time he skipped class in high school, stole a motorcycle off a showroom floor, and crashed it into a lake. Word on the street was that his father was the one who put him in a weeklong coma, not the accident itself.

Cross sits to my left, his Zippo in his hand. He keeps flipping the lid open and then closed. It's not a tic, just something he has done since grade school. The guy is obsessed with fire. He lights things up just to watch them burn and gets a sick pleasure from it. I remember our senior year. Things took a turn when ...

"I'm guessing it went well," Bones interrupts my thoughts.

I look over at him sitting at the head of the table. His tatted forearms, covering up part of Kingdom written in gold. Bones got his name in middle school. An older kid picked on his younger brother, Grave. Bones beat the shit out of him right then and there in the hallway. Broke twenty bones with his hands. I've liked him ever since.

"It did," I answer, reaching forward and unzipping the suitcase. Pushing the top open, it slaps the conference table. I grab a brick of hundred-dollar bills.

Titan arches a brow. "That better be half."

I grab another and toss it beside the other. "Two bricks," I inform them. A brick of hundred-dollar bills is one hundred thousand dollars, and I just gave them two. Leaving them with fifty grand each. "Thanks for the tip."

Then I reach into the suitcase and grab two dime bags and toss them over to Grave. He catches them midair. "A little extra."

He gives me a smile before placing his treat in the pocket of his holey jeans. I take care of Grave, and he takes care of me.

Bones clears his throat, letting me know he disapproves that I just gave his younger brother some drugs, but I don't give a fuck. We're all adults here, and we all have our vices.

He places his palms flat on the smooth surface and stands. "We're done here."

I nod and zip up the suitcase. "As always, it was a pleasure doing business with you, Kings."

Grave smiles, and my brother laughs.

I nod and turn to Titan. "Tell your queen I said thanks for the information."

He nods. "Anytime."

I pick up the suitcase when Grave speaks. "How is the wedding coming along?"

I smile at him. They know my plan. Have known for a

few months. I filled them in because they can benefit from it too. "As well as predicted."

"Ah, come on, man, she can't hate you that much," he jokes, but I don't laugh because the truth is my soon-to-be wife hates me with a passion, and if I cared at all I'd call it off.

Just to clear things up, I don't care, and the wedding is still very much on.

"Aren't all weddings like that?" Cross asks.

Titan snorts. "Fuck that shit."

"Not like she had a choice," my brother chimes in, still chewing on that damn toothpick.

The Kings know our life and how things work. Theirs aren't run much differently. But where marriage gives us power, they all see it as a disadvantage. Being tied to one woman all their life would be horror. To me, it means millions in my pocket. And I don't pass up money. Ever.

"I look forward to the engagement party." Grave laughs.

I PULL MY CAR INTO MY GARAGE AND TURN IT OFF, then grab the flowers out of my passenger seat that I picked up on the way home. Thankfully, my favorite florist was open.

I exit my car and walk into the house. It's quiet, and I know she's not here. She's on her morning run. The sun is just starting to rise. She likes to start her day off early with a run to free her mind. At least she used to. She didn't ask me for permission, but this house isn't a prison. She can come and go all she wants. I have guards all over it. Cameras at every corner. If she decides to leave me, she won't get far. I don't think she'd chance her freedom. If she did, she wouldn't like the consequences that would follow.

Walking into one of the many kitchens, I grab a vase from underneath the sink and fill it with water before placing the flowers in it. It's been a long time since I've used it. The last time was before I left her. When she used to stay here, she always made the house feel like a home. It's been silent and empty ever since.

Making my way up to our master suite, I close the door after entering. The bed is freshly made, and the smell of her perfume hits me. I used to smell her on me for days. The way her shampoo would rub off on my shirt when she cuddled up against me. Or the way my hoodie would smell like her body wash. It always made me hard. Desperate.

She doesn't know it, but I forced her father to hand her over to me. I'm not the kind of guy who shows weakness. My father taught my brothers and me that nothing is more important than money. And although I agree, I also feel that having a woman by your side can be beneficial to a man. Men respect a man who knows how to control a bitch. I needed her, and I needed a reason to make that happen. My father didn't agree, but he'll come around. He'll see what I see in the end. And if not, well, then that's his problem.

The moment I stepped on that plane to leave her for Italy, I started forming a plan. It was the first thing I did three months ago when I arrived back in the States. Her father owns a chain of banks here in Las Vegas, and I could use his facilities to launder money. All I had to do was make him an offer he couldn't refuse.

HE SITS BEHIND HIS DESK IN HIS HOME OFFICE, HIS HANDS clenched together as he glares at me. "What you're asking of me is illegal."

"And what you're doing is illegal."

His face whitens and sweat beads across his forehead. "I don't know ..."

"You're running fake money through your bank. Marking it with serial numbers from real currency. Making it look like it's being placed in the vault, but instead you're using it to hold your head above water."

His jaw sharpens. "You have no idea—"

"I do," I interrupt him. "You have rats everywhere." I smile at him. "Especially when they're paid well." Lie. I got this information for free. But I promised not to snitch on my source. And the Bianchis are no rats.

He slams his hand down on the desk and stands.

I stay seated because I'm about to cut him off at the knees. "I'll make you one offer. And it will only be on the table for twenty-four hours."

His jaw clenches, but he doesn't shoot me down immediately. "The board will never allow it."

"Let me worry about the board." Standing, I button my suit jacket. "You will allow me full rein of all fifteen locations in exchange for twenty percent of my incoming finances. And in the meantime, I won't rat you out to the feds."

He falls into his chair and lets out a sigh. He's thinking about it. Good. It's a fair offer. I'm not gonna railroad him because I want something else of his as well.

He concedes, releasing a long breath. "I'll see what I can do."

"And I want Haven."

"What?" he snaps, jumping back to his feet. "Absolutely not!"

I snap my fingers. "Nite." He walks over and drops the black bag on top of the desk. "Open it," I order Jimmy.

He arches a brow, staring down at it, but eventually, his curiosity gets the better of him, and he unzips it. He pulls out stacks of hundreds. "What ...?"

"In exchange for her hand in marriage, I will give you five million dollars."

"Marriage?" he whispers softly as if he can't say it out loud, but the way his eyes light up at the cash he grips in his hands tells me I've already won. He's in deep debt. So what if he sells his only child? His adopted child? She doesn't mean anything to him. Not like she does me.

"I'll let you think about it." I turn, letting him keep what little money is in there right now while he thinks about it. As I place my hand on the doorknob, he speaks.

"Wait."

I bite back a smile, turning to face him.

He stands there, both hands gripping a stack of money, and his chest heaves in his tight button-down. But his eyes tell me all I need to know. She's mine.

THAT WAS THREE MONTHS AGO. I NEEDED THINGS TO BE set in place because I couldn't just go and grab her. Papers needed to be signed, and I needed access to all the locations before I stepped in and removed her from her home. I needed my ducks in a row. She was the last one because I knew she would be the only one to fight me.

But in the end, she would lose.

And it didn't take more than a few days for him to come

around. He was practically drooling when I handed him the money and couldn't get her to sign fast enough.

I turn off the shower and step out. Wrapping the towel around my hips, I walk back into the bedroom just as I hear commotion downstairs.

Making my way to the first level, I walk into the spare bedroom, listening to the shower turn on in the adjoining bathroom. I enter and see her removing her sports bra and then shoving the sweaty yoga pants down her thin legs. And I have to fight the urge to shove her to her knees and fuck her mouth. She always gave great head. The woman knew how to use that mouth. Even if at times I wanted to duct tape the damn thing shut.

I'm not sure why she's being such a bitch now. I paid for her. Her father was the one who tossed her to the side. I want to make her my queen and give her anything she wants. All she has to do is ask, but I'm starting to lose my patience. And that is not a good thing for her. She's going to push me to the point I'll no longer give a fuck, and then she'll hate me even more.

She stiffens when her eyes meet mine in the large bathroom mirror.

I push off the wall and walk up behind her. Placing my hands on her narrow hips, I lean down and kiss her bare shoulder. She glares at me in the mirror.

"Good morning, Haven," I whisper, and I feel her body shiver.

She wants me. She always has. I've been able to push her in ways that no other guy could. Ever since I saw her in grade school, I wanted her. She wasn't like all the other girls who wanted to be seen with me. She didn't care one bit.

"I bought you flowers." I gather up her mess of hair into

my fist. I run my lips across the top of her back to her other shoulder, softly kissing her damp skin.

"Flowers die," she growls.

I smile against her skin. "Would you prefer diamonds?"

"Diamonds were just once coal," she bites out.

"How about orgasms?" I ask, tightening my fist in her hair and pulling her head back. My free hand slides around her skinny waist and dips between her legs.

She pushes me off her and spins around to face me. "Luca ..."

I slam my lips to hers, cutting her off, and grind my hips into hers. The movement has the knot holding my towel on loosening and falling to the floor at our feet.

She opens for me, a moan escaping her lips before I swallow it. My free hand comes up and grips her chin, arching her neck back for me. I deepen the kiss, just as the palms of her hands hit my chest.

She steps away from me, breathing heavily, and shouts, "I said no." There's that fire I like. But it's unnecessary at the moment. I'm not the one she should be mad at.

"I never heard those words."

She slaps me across the face. "I'm not for sale, Luca. I'm not going to give you my body because you wrote a check."

"It was actually cash ..."

She slaps me again.

This time, I grip her face, spin her around, and slam her back into the wall. Her eyes widen, and she gasps. Her hands come up and grip my wrists. "Luca ..."

"Let's get one thing straight, Haven," I growl in her face. "We can do this one of two ways. One, you cooperate, and I'll treat you well. Or two, you be a fucking bitch, and I treat you like one. Do you understand me?"

Her pretty, dark eyes fill with tears. I watch one fall

down her flushed cheek from her run. She's so beautiful. She always was. When other girls were spending hours on their makeup, she was throwing on mascara and lip gloss and called it good. She has a little freckle on the right side of her upper lip, and I loved to run my thumb over it. Her amber-colored eyes and chestnut hair make her stunning. She is what a man dreams of. I know I always have. That's why I never let her get too far away. There were many times she tried to break it off with me, but I wouldn't let her. I am Luca Bianchi, and I always get what I want. Even if I have to lie, cheat, or steal for it. She will be my wife and the mother of my children.

"Luca," she whimpers.

"Do you understand?" I shout, losing my patience. I don't know why she's fighting me on this. She should be thanking me. I saved her father. Her future. She would be out on the streets with them within a year at the rate he was going. He's in deep debt and was about to lose everything before I stepped in. They were days away from their Victorian mansion being in foreclosure. Her father had several of his cars hidden in an undisclosed lot, for Christ's sake. What would she have done? Where would she have gone?

"Yes," she whispers as the tears run down her face.

I release her and take a step back. Not even bothering to grab my towel, I exit the bathroom and slam the door shut behind me. I pass by the kitchen, grab the flowers, and throw them into the trash, knowing that I need to show Haven just what kind of a guy I can be.

HAVEN

I STAND IN the bathroom, silently crying, trying to get my emotions under control. My run didn't help one bit.

74

And neither did last night. I couldn't sleep. He had walked out of his room and never returned.

Where the hell had he gone? Who did he go meet? Was it a woman? I hate how much I care to know the answer to that question. And he had recently showered. His hair was wet, and his towel sits at my feet. I lean down to pick it up. Had he showered to get the smell of a woman off? Did he use protection?

We both know we're not marrying for love, so it wouldn't surprise me to know he spent the night with someone else.

I open the shower door and turn on the water. I step in and allow the scalding hot water to burn my skin. To cover my tears. What will my life be now? How long until he gets bored with me? Before he throws me away? I didn't get to read the contract. Did it have a clause where we have to stay married for so many years? And if so, how many? I don't know a lot about the Mafia, but I'm pretty sure the only way you can be free is if they die. And even after that, your life is still devoted to the Mafia.

I take my time in the shower, making sure to scrub every inch of my body. At one point, I sit down and rock back and forth, trying to come up with a plan. But I get nothing.

My name has been signed. The deal is done.

Stepping out, I wrap the towel around myself and walk into the spare bedroom. I scream when I see a man standing over by the door.

I tighten the towel around myself. "What are you doing? Get out!" I shout.

He doesn't move, doesn't even look at me. It's Nite, standing there like a fucking statue. "Get the fuck out!" I scream.

He ignores me like he always has. Huffing, I storm over

to the door and yank it open. I run up the stairs and into Luca's bedroom. I hear water running in the bathroom, and I yank it open. He stands at one of the sinks, bent over, his hands splashing his face with water.

He straightens, gripping the towel and yanking it off the hanger next to him, and wipes his face. His eyes meet mine in the mirror. "What do you want, Haven?" he asks with a growl.

My jaw tightens. "I want you to get Nite out of my fucking room."

"No."

"No?" I gasp. "Is this a joke?"

He turns to face me, and I stand my ground as his eyes bore into mine. "This is very real, Haven. Nite will accompany you at all times from now on."

"Luca ..."

"And no more morning runs."

"You can't be serious?" I growl. He's going to make me a prisoner. His plaything that will only be meant to satisfy him in the bedroom. The other ninety-five percent of the time, he will run around on me with whoever he pleases whenever he wants. We're going to be just like his parents.

He shoulders past me and back into his bedroom but doesn't answer me.

"Luca?" I snap as he enters his walk-in closet.

He stands with his back to me in nothing but a pair of black boxer briefs. He removes a black button-down from a hanger and shrugs it on.

"I'm talking to you," I seethe.

He removes a pair of black slacks from another hanger and goes to step into them.

I yank them from his hands. "Listen to me."

"I don't listen to nonsense," he says calmly and takes the slacks back before sliding them on.

I stand before him, stunned. My heart pounding with anger and my jaw tight. I watch him tuck his shirt in and then button them up along with the zipper. And I wonder what he's doing. Where he's going. I had only gone for a thirty-minute run, and he wasn't here when I left. I checked like the sorry piece of shit woman I am. A million different scenarios went through my mind. All of them involved a woman and him in bed together.

"Leaving already?" I ask, crossing my arms over my chest. He wants me to be his wife? I can be the most annoying, intrusive, demanding wife possible. He'll want to pay someone to take me off his hands.

He looks up at me. His brow creases at my question. After a long beat, he answers, "I have work to do."

Cryptic. No surprise there. "Work or someone?"

The corners of his lips turn up, and my breath hitches. *Why did I ask that?*

He takes the five steps, closing the short distance between us. Reaching up, he pushes my wet hair from my face and tucks it behind my ear. "Are you jealous, Haven?"

I snort at the question, but my heart is now racing because it's true. The thought of him with other women has haunted me ever since he left me for Italy. Now he's going to openly do it in front of me. "No."

"Liar." He wraps his arm around my towel, pulling me to him. His other hand tangles in my wet hair. "I'll tell you what." He lowers his lips to my ear, and I hold my breath. "How about you fall to your knees and suck my dick to try to keep me faithful?"

I try to pull back, but he keeps me captive. "You son of a—"

"You remember how I like it?" he interrupts me, his hand yanking my head back and forcing me to look up at him with tears in my eyes. I refuse to let them fall. Letting go of my waist, he runs the pad of his thumb over my bottom lip. His eyes boring into mine. I see the amusement in his. He's enjoying this, and it's breaking my heart. "You were always so good at opening that mouth for me when I wanted it."

My hands fist his freshly pressed button-down, hoping I wrinkle the fuck out of it. "You're not the only one I got on my knees for," I say, hoping to fucking shatter any thoughts he has of me. I want this fucker to hate me as much as I hate him. Even if I have to lie.

His face grows as hard as stone, and his eyes narrow on me. I can feel his body stiffen as he holds me tighter. Closer. I don't dare move. Or breathe. We glare at one another. I wait to see what he does next because I know he contemplates snapping my neck.

Thankfully, the door opens, and he shoves me away. I look up to see Nite enter the massive walk-in closet. He holds out his right hand to Luca.

My eyes widen. "Is that my phone?" I ask. Did that fucker dig through my purse to retrieve it? He had to. It was on the bed downstairs ...

"Thanks, Nite," Luca says tightly and then places the phone in the pocket of his slacks.

"Hey, that's mine."

Nite nods and exits the room, closing the door behind him.

Luca turns to me. "Nothing here is yours. Everything belongs to me. Even you." Then he too turns and exits the room, slamming the door shut behind him.

FIVE

LUCA

I SIT IN the driver's seat of my car, scrolling through her phone. She didn't have a lock on it, so it made this easier. I go through all her texts, calls coming and going, and nothing shows any sign of a guy that I can see. Everything consists of her friends, Emilee and Jasmine.

I go through her pictures. She doesn't have many. They're mostly of her and Jasmine. A few of her and Emilee.

Turning the phone off, I throw it onto the passenger seat and run a hand down my face. I've never felt so fucking jealous, so furious with her in my life. I wanted to strangle her. The thought of her touching another guy, let alone on her knees for another sends me into a rage. I'm going to find out who it is, and I'm going to break his goddamn legs.

Pulling my own cell out of my pocket, I shoot Nite a text.

Me: Don't let her out of your sight.

He answers immediately.

Yes, sir.

Her little stunt in the bathroom earlier earned her a babysitter. She wants to act like a kid, then I'll treat her like one.

Thirty minutes later, I'm pulling into a parking lot right off the Strip. *Glass* in black letters is written on the side of the two-story building. I make my way around to the back and park next to a blacked-out Lamborghini Reventon. Only thirty-five were made in the world, and my business partner owns one of them.

Exiting my car, I walk up the metal staircase to the second floor and punch in the code on the keypad to unlock the door. I step inside and walk down the hallway, entering the first door on the right.

I walk over to the desk and drop Haven's cell on top of it, right in front of my business partner.

His brows pull together as he looks at the picture of Haven and Emilee from when she went to visit her three months ago in Chicago. She doesn't know that I know. But she hasn't done a damn thing without my knowledge. That's why I don't understand how she could have been seeing someone and I missed it. She had to have been lying. And when I find out that's the case, she will regret making up shit just to rile me up.

"What's this about?" Bones asks, leaning back in his seat.

"Haven's phone."

He arches a brow. "And?"

"And nothing." I sit down in the chair.

He reaches up and shoves the phone away. I smile to myself. He never speaks of Emilee, but that doesn't mean he's forgotten about her. You don't ever forget the one who got away. Or more like the one you let go of.

"What couldn't wait until later?" I ask. The bastard called me an hour ago and said to meet him here. I had planned on going home and getting a few hours of sleep, but he doesn't care about things like that. He and Titan rarely sleep. They only crawl into a bed if it's to fuck a woman.

"Marco is on his way," he answers.

"Ah." I nod. "What do we plan on doing to him?"

"Not sure yet."

So we could be burying a body in the desert in the next hour or not. Never know with Bones. Just depends on what kind of mood you catch him in.

Just then, the door opens, and the man of the hour enters. He doesn't look like he's been to bed yet either. He wears a pair of black jeans and a red collared shirt. It's the dress code here at Glass for the male employees.

He looks from me to Bones and comes to a halt. "Bones?" he shrieks.

Everyone in Las Vegas knows the Dark Kings. They're each feared for something different. Bones is known as the enforcer, but no one knows that he owns a part of Glass. He's a silent business partner. So Marco probably thinks I hired him to work him over. Get his hands dirty for me.

"Have a seat." I gesture to the chair I vacated.

"No, that's okay ..."

I grab his shirt and shove him down into it.

Bones grabs the remote, pointing it at the large monitor that hangs on the wall, and then pushes play.

The date in the lower right-hand corner shows three weeks ago. You see Marco working behind the bar, rushing around making drinks. Then you see the customer give him cash. He slips some in his back pocket and only rings up half of the cocktails he just made.

Bones pauses it. "I have fifteen more just like this."

"I can explain ..."

"We don't need an explanation," Bones says. "See ..." He places his tatted hands flat on the desk "The only thing I care about is money. And you owe us five grand."

"I ... I can ... I'll ..."

"You'll pay us back," I say.

He nods quickly and begins to dig in his pocket. He throws some twenties on the desk. "That's everything I have on me." He quickly pats his other pockets to double-check.

Bones ignores the money and grabs a blank piece of paper from the printer. He sets it on the desk along with a pen. "Sign this."

"What?" Marco blinks.

"I said sign it."

"But there's nothing there." His round eyes look it over.

There's a tic in Bones jaw. "If you don't sign your name on this, I will break both of your hands. Do you understand?"

The guy grabs the pen and scribbles his name down.

"You have five days to come up with the money," he says, falling back down into his seat.

Marco nods, jumps up, and storms out without another word. He doesn't have to be told twice.

The door slams shut, and Bones leans his head back, closing his eyes.

"Go home. Get some rest," I tell him. "You look like shit."

He runs a hand down his unshaven face. "I'm heading to Kingdom."

No one knows about our business deal here. Two years

ago, I went to Bones with a plan. I wanted to start a business that didn't involve my father. I wanted something that was completely mine. Something I had control over. I had the perfect place and the money. I just needed someone to help me with it while I was in Italy. A partner.

Bones was the perfect candidate.

So we went into business together and bought Glass, a strip club right in the heart of Sin City. It was once a run-down wedding chapel, so it felt fitting.

The girls are the elite of Vegas strippers. They must be at least twenty-one and audition, but other than that, they can pretty much do whatever the fuck they want. We have VIP rooms. The men pay for bottle service, and the girls decide how far they want to take it. We make sure the girls are taken care of and well protected. We always have armed guards on the property. Plus, most of them also work as a queen at Kingdom. They're literally rolling in cash.

His phone rings, and he digs it out of his pocket. Hitting answer, he leans back in the chair. "Hello?" He pauses. "Yeah, I'm about to head that way." He runs a hand down his face again. "I'll take care of it." Then he hangs up and stands. "I gotta go. Make sure Marco pays up. If not, let me know, and I'll deliver the threat."

HAVEN

I sɪᴛ ᴏᴜᴛ on a chaise on the large balcony to *our* room. Nite stands off to the side by the sliding glass door. True to Luca's word, the bastard has been breathing down my neck ever since this morning. I look over the black railing at the heart of Sin City. You can see the Strip from where the house sits. I always found Las Vegas ugly and dirty during the day, but at night, it comes to life and shines brighter than all the stars in the sky.

Standing out the most, Kingdom, dominates the sky with four towers—one for each king. Back when their fathers owned it, it only had two. They've built onto it over the years. When they took over after college, they made some changes. And those alterations made them even more untouchable. More royalty in this town. And gave them even more enemies.

I take a puff from my cigarette. Leaning my head back, I let it out slowly and close my eyes, thinking of Emilee and how much I miss her. I visited her recently in Chicago.

"So what are we gonna do while I'm in town?" I ask, falling onto her bed. Her entire apartment is about as big as her bedroom back home, but she doesn't seem to mind. Emilee never needed expensive things.

She walks out of her bathroom and gives me a big smile. "We're going out tonight."

"Where to?"

"A club."

"That's vague."

She winks at me.

I laugh because I love seeing her like this. So free. Bones always had a hold on her. She swore she didn't love him, and I believed her, but the Kings were two years older than us. So when Bones, Titan, and Cross graduated, they started to take over Kingdom, and that left Emilee alone. She has never said it out loud, but I know that hurt her. They grew apart, and she started seeing someone in our grade. After graduation, she chose to move to Chicago, and that was that. She was gone. I think she was running away from something she knew she couldn't have. None of the Kings would ever settle down. They were meant to be ruthless playboys who ruled their own world and had no room for women or families.

"There's this awesome club here called Seven Deadly Sins."

"Oh, I like it already."

She nods. "They have these private rooms for each sin."

"Sounds fun."

"It is by far the best club I've ever been to."

I eye her skeptically as she smooths down her dress in the floor-length mirror. She turns around and looks at her ass over her shoulder. "You're fucking someone who works there." It was more of a statement than a question.

She chuckles "I am. I'll message him before we get there, and he'll let us in the back."

"It is serious?" I ask. I've known Emilee all my life, and I've never seen her fall in love with a guy. I don't know if she just hides her emotions that well, or if she truly can just use a guy. Maybe Bones broke her.

I hate that I've only ever slept with Luca, and that I can't get over the fact I love him so much. I want to be more like her. Detached.

She frowns. "No, it's just a little fun."

"What does he do at the club? What's his name? I wanna know all about him."

THE GUY TURNED OUT TO BE A PRETTY NICE GUY. NOT to mention gorgeous in that I'll kick anyone's ass kind of way. I could totally understand why he was head of security. We got to watch him in action twice that night.

He put us up in one of the rooms with a waitress who kept the drinks flowing all night. After the club closed, we went out and ate breakfast with him. Then he drove us back to Emilee's apartment. I went inside while he kissed her goodbye on her porch—I might have watched out the window—and then he left. We stayed up a few more hours laughing and sharing a bottle of Riesling she had until we made our way down to the closest gas station and bought a pack of cigarettes. We had only ever smoked one other time in college. For some reason, we both thought it would be a great idea to try it again.

She didn't care that much for it, so I put them in my suitcase. The same ones that were packed and brought here to Luca's. We were drunk and really didn't know what we were doing then, but I light one up every now and then.

Keeping my eyes shut, I take another drag of the cigarette. I miss her so much and wish that she were here. Hell, I wish I could talk to her. Luca may have taken my cell away, but I found a phone in his study earlier today. I waited for Nite to stop me, but when he didn't, I dialed her number. She didn't answer, and I didn't leave a voicemail. What would I say? *Hey, E. I've been forced to marry Luca, and I wish you were here to help me through it?* I just hung up.

"What in the fuck are you doing?"

My eyes spring open, and I jump at the sound of his voice. "Luca ..."

"Since when did you start fucking smoking?" he demands, his blue eyes narrowed on the cigarette between my fingers.

I bring it to my lips. "I do a lot of things you don't know about."

He snatches it from my fingers and puts it out on the railing.

"Hey!"

He grips my upper arm, pulling me from the balcony and through the open door into his bedroom. My eyes fall to the massive bed that sits up against the wall with it's white comforter and burgundy sheets. And I think of how many women he's had there, and I hate it. I hate that he makes me jealous and that he's brought me here in the first place.

"Let go of me." I try yanking my arm free of his hold, but he just grips me tighter.

He walks over to a door, yanks it open, and shoves me inside. I spin around to face him just as he shoves it closed in Nite's face.

Fisting my hands, I turn to see we're in a closet. He shoulders past me, walking down the short and narrow structure, then he takes a left and disappears. Rubbing my upper arm, I follow him. I've always dreamed of my things being in here. Now I want to burn my shit so I don't have to fill it. We make the turn, and it opens to a large room. The left side is full of white shelves from the floor to the ceiling. Ahead of me are different-sized cubbies with rods to hang clothes on in various sizes. It looks the same but different.

In the middle is a silver dresser with a glass top. Running my hands over it, I smudge the glass with my fingers. We had sex on it once. It has three large drawers. Walking around the other side, I open the top drawer. It's long but not very deep. It's covered in black velvet, and the indentions let me know it's for jewelry. I pause when I spot the Harry Winston three-carat emerald sitting in a platinum setting on the fifth row. It looks out of place.

My mouth instantly goes dry, and I take a step back, shaking my head slowly. Luca reaches in and grabs the ring and turns to face me. Tears sting my eyes as he grabs my left hand. I want to punch him. Fight him. I want to tell him that it's ugly and over the top, but it's really all I ever wanted.

He slides it on my finger, and a tear slides down my face. It fits perfectly, of course. He runs his finger over it before releasing my hand. It drops to my side like an anchor, the weight pulling my hand down.

I spin around to run, but something else stops me. My stomach drops when I see the black garment bag hanging from the rack. I take a step back, but my ass hits the dresser. "Is that ...?" I swallow the knot in my throat. It's a reminder of what this truly is.

A contract.

This isn't love.

The ring. The dress. It's all too much. Too fast. There has to be a way to stop it.

He comes up to me and places his hands on either side of my hips. I stiffen.

"Calm down, Haven," he orders softly. "I can hear your heart pounding in your chest."

I feel it may explode.

"This is your dress for our engagement announcement tonight."

That doesn't help me. Just because it's not a wedding dress doesn't mean it's not just as threatening.

He runs his knuckles down the side of my face, smearing the single tear down my neck. He stops on my racing pulse, and I look up at him. "We can ... You can call it off." I stumble over my words. "It's never too late."

He arches a brow.

My heart pounds as my thumb runs over the platinum band of my engagement ring. "They don't get to rule our lives. I know—"

"They?" he interrupts me.

Swallowing nervously, I add, "Our fathers."

He gives me a smile that makes the hairs on my neck stand. He opens his hand and slides it into my hair, tilting my head back in the process. I hold my breath as he bends down and whispers in my ear, "This is all my doing, Haven. Make no mistake about that. I wanted you, and now I have you. Today, tomorrow, forever." He kisses my forehead gently. When he pulls away, I feel another tear fall. His dark eyes watch it without any remorse. "Get in the shower. You smell like cigarette smoke. And Mrs. Brown will be here in an hour to help you get ready." With that, he exits the closet.

The sound of the door shutting behind me has me falling to my knees.

SIX

HAVEN

I STAND IN the middle of the ballroom at Luca's. He stands to my right, my father to my left. They both have smiles on their faces and laugh at the stupid jokes the men tell.

I feel numb, completely and utterly numb. I've thought of taking one of the butter knives that the waiters carry around on their trays and stabbing myself in the chest just to see if I feel it. I wonder how long it takes a person to bleed out? Maybe my best option would be to go for a wrist. Would they be quick enough to stop me? Would they be smart enough to stop the bleeding? Most likely. Everyone knows to put pressure on a wound. But if I could cut it deep enough …

I've never contemplated suicide until tonight. But I have come to a point in my life where that may be the only way out. Death has always been this black cloud hovering over us all, but at this point, it may be my saving grace.

It's our engagement party. The announcement of our engagement. Luca's mansion is full of reporters, mob bosses, the Mafia, and my father's clients. Complete strangers to me.

Jasmine isn't here because I haven't spoken to her. And I haven't had a chance to try to call Emilee again. I'm all alone.

"Haven?" Luca growls my name in my ear and tightens his hand on my hip. He's had me glued to his side all night, showing me off like a trophy he won. "Mr. Ronald asked you a question."

I blink. "I'm so sorry." And fake a smile. I feel my face may crack due to how tight it is.

The man with the biggest gap I've ever seen between his teeth looks straight at my tits. I'm not surprised. Mrs. Brown did my hair and makeup, then dressed me in a pink Chanel dress that zips up the back. It comes up high on my neck like a noose but has a keyhole front, dipping low to show off my cleavage.

The dress Luca bought for me. I no longer have any say on how I look or what I wear.

Luca controls me. I'm his puppet. His toy. Something to show off in a forty-thousand-dollar dress. When he saw me, he said I looked absolutely stunning. Breathtaking. It makes me look like a fucking hooker. Not that I'm judging them. Just wish I was getting something out of this.

Mr. Ronald clears his throat, and the guy lifts his eyes from my chest. "Yes, my dear. I just wanted to congratulate you." He holds out his right hand.

Thoughtlessly, I reach out and shake it. "Thank you." My voice is monotone. He says a few more words to Luca and then walks away. My shoulders instantly sag.

"Can you be more ... believable?" My father huffs, straightening his suit jacket.

My chest tightens at his words. What did I do to

deserve this? Have I made him ashamed? Is this his way of forcing me to make something of my life? Or a way to further his career? He's very successful. I thought he and Mr. Bianchi put this together, but Luca told me earlier today that it was all him. But it has to be more than that. My father wouldn't throw me away like I'm nothing unless he had a hand in it.

"I need a drink," I say, pulling away from between them.

"Nonalcoholic," Luca warns.

I keep my expression blank, but I'm screaming at him on the inside. Lifting the hem of my dress off the floor, I make my way down the long hallway to the formal dining area. I pass through it to the back and look around before I push open the revolving door to the commercial-size kitchen.

Workers run around with trays in their hands. Cooks are standing at the massive grills. And there's an assembly line of people preparing plates. I walk through, and nobody even gives me a glance, too busy with keeping up with Luca's demanding orders. Shoving the back door open, I walk down the long and dark narrow hallway, looking over my shoulder to make sure I'm not being followed. I come to the end and turn the handle. Closing it softly behind me, I flip the light switch that I know is on the wall, which lights up the staircase and room below.

I lift my dress once again and walk down the stairs, my heels clicking on the wood. I smile once I hit the landing. Going over to the bottles of wine, I pick the one I want and then turn to the cabinet that has a wine opener. After opening it, I don't even bother to look for a glass. I tip back the bottle and down it like it's a shot, not even caring that it's warm.

93

I don't know how much time passes before I push myself up off the floor, toss the now empty bottle into the trash, and fumble up the stairs. I trip twice on my dress. Opening the door, I'm much less quiet as I make my way back down the hall and back through the kitchen to the party. No one pays me any attention, though. I'm not the reason they're here. All four hundred people are here for Luca. For his future. For his business. I'm no one. Nothing. But that's how women are treated in this world. The Mafia is an exclusive men's club. The women stay home and raise the children, most of the time in a Catholic upbringing. I know nothing about the religion. I've never even entered a church because my parents aren't religious. Is he going to make me do research? Or make his mother teach me? Was that mentioned in the contract that I didn't read?

"Haven?"

I stop in my tracks at the sound of her voice. *My mother.* The woman who has successfully avoided me.

I turn to see her approaching me in a champagne-colored sleeveless Burberry dress. Her bleach blond hair is up in a tight bun, showcasing her delicate neck and the pearls my father gave her for Christmas last year. She looks stunning, as always, and for the first time in my life, I feel nothing but hatred toward her. Where was she when my father signed my name to the contract? Where was she when Nite removed me from my parents' house? And where has she been for the past couple of days while I've been a prisoner here?

She brings her hands up to her face and gasps as she looks me up and down. "You look beautiful. Absolutely stunning." She reaches out for my hand, but I take a stumbling step back from her. And her perfectly painted on face falls as if I hurt her feelings. "Haven, I—"

"I don't care," I interrupt her, then hiccup.

Her green eyes fall to my left hand, and she stares at the rock on my finger. She flinches as if it hurts her to see. She should put herself in my shoes, then maybe she would know how much it hurts to wear it. "Haven, please let me explain."

"How you let Daddy sell me?" She flinches at my slurred speech. "No thanks."

Her eyes dart around the room to see if anyone heard me, but I highly doubt those in attendance believe I chose this. "Haven, please ...?"

"Go home, *Mother*." I turn, giving her my back. Walking out of the formal dining room, I head down the hallway to the back of his house where the bedroom I've been staying in is at. I have nothing to say to her. What my father did hurt, but my mother didn't even try to save me. Not once has she tried to call me in the two days I've been here. That I know of. Now Luca has my phone. She let me go. And that's a hard pill to swallow. She was supposed to protect me. Love me. Instead, she let him throw me away.

"Haven. Well, don't you look every bit the part of a princess."

I stiffen as I come face to face with Brad. He's Bones and Grave's father. He used to run Kingdom until his sons and their friends were old enough to take over the empire. He's the only living member of the Three Wisemen who created Kingdom.

His blue eyes look me up and down in a way that makes me step back. I never liked him. He's dirty, evil just like the rest of them. He uses women. All he cares about is how much money he can make and who will fall to their knees and suck his dick.

He leans in, giving me a smile. "Don't worry, your secret

95

is safe with me. I won't tell anyone that this isn't the fairy tale you wanted."

Without saying a word, I narrow my eyes and shoulder past him. I just want to be alone. Locked inside my bedroom where no one can bother me. Continuing down the hallway, I come to a stop when Luca's office door opens, and a woman steps out. Before she has a chance to see me, I duck into a nearby half bathroom, watching her through the thin crack in the door, hiding my body behind it. She runs her hands down her black form-fitting dress, shoving it down her long legs. But it doesn't cover much. She's dressed more for a night out on the town. Then she steps up to the large mirror that hangs on the wall and fixes her wild, bleach blond hair. It's knotted around the crown. Like someone's fist was in it. She opens her clutch and reapplies her crimson lipstick, before popping her lips. I look over her arms and see red marks have formed on her pale skin. Fingerprints. She looks herself over one last time and then turns.

I move away from the door, hoping she doesn't see me. Placing my hand over my mouth, I hold my breath so she can't hear me as I listen for her heels on the hardwood as she passes my hiding place.

I wait for her to walk off, and I look out the cracked door. Once I see I'm alone, I yank it open, storm down the hall, and all but kick his office door open.

A large TV hangs on the far wall above a fireplace. Over to the right sits his desk. He has some papers scattered across the surface. I walk across the room, my heels digging into the thick black rug. I sit down and read them over. My eyes are a tad blurry from the alcohol swirling around in my system, but something catches my eyes on the third page. I recognize it. It's the paperwork where my father signed my name. There's a blood stain through the middle of Haven.

This isn't a marriage. It's a contract signed in blood.

I read over it, trying to comprehend it. With blurry vision, it's hard to understand, but one word catches my attention. Heirs.

My hands begin to shake as I blink to focus.

The wife in question will produce three living heirs. Two of which must be sons.

All cases after that will be up to Luca's discretion.

What the fuck does that mean?

I place the papers on the desk, my head falling into my hands. My eyes drop to the small black trash can under his desk. Something catches my eye, and I pick up the small container. "What the fuck?" I whisper.

My blood begins to boil, and my heart pounds. I hear the lock to the adjoining bathroom click, and then Luca steps out. He comes to a stop when he spots me. My eyes immediately drop to his black slacks. His belt is undone along with his pants and his white button-down is untucked. His black tie hangs loosely around his neck.

"What are you doing in here?" he asks, his eyes narrowing when they drop to the papers.

"What were you doing in here?" I snap, unable to hold my tongue.

"Haven ...."

"Explain this!" I shout, dumping the trashcan upside down and allowing the contents to scatter on his desk. We'll get back to the paperwork later. Right now, we're not even having sex, let alone having children, but he's fucking someone. The freshly used condom falls onto the contract. Might as well mix some cum with that bloody signature. "You were just fucking her in here!" I scream.

That's why the blonde was in his office. She fixed herself in the mirror while he freshened up in his bathroom.

My breath quickens, heart races, and my hands clench. I shouldn't be mad. Or jealous. I don't want to be his, not like this. But like my father said, the deal is done. The bloodstained signature that sits underneath the used condom proves that.

A smirk grows across his face as if this is some kind of joke. "I left you a present." He goes to reach into his unzipped slacks. "I know how much you like to lick me clean."

My entire body stiffens at what he's implying. I want to fucking stab him in the eyes, but this is how he was raised. This is what his life has taught him about how women should be treated, but I won't do it. "I'm not a Mafia whore," I spit out. "I will not be some fucking trophy for you to parade around in public while you fuck around behind my back." I pick up a glass paperweight and throw it at his head, cussing when I miss him by a mile. Damn drunk aim. I would have been spot-on if I was sober.

His eyes darken, jaw sharpens, and chest bows. I take a step back from his desk. He reaches out, grabbing the netting on my dress, and yanks me forward, making my chest bump into his. "You're mine," he growls in my face.

I begin to tremble as his words penetrate my foggy brain.

"I own every inch of you now."

"I hate you," I croak out.

He releases me and runs his knuckles down the side of my face. I whimper at his soft touch, waiting for him to hit me. Do whatever he wants with me to beat me into submission. His eyes drill into mine. "Would you rather it had been you bent over that desk?"

"I will never willingly lie down for you again." I lift my chin even though I want to burst into tears.

His knuckles run lower, tracing my jaw and then my neck. I know he can feel my pulse race. Fuck, I'm panting with fear. Mafia men only marry for one reason—a baby. An heir. We may have talked about marriage in the past, but we never discussed children. And that paperwork proves he's thought of everything. I should have seen it and realized it sooner. He doesn't love me. He never did. He just wants to use me. "I won't give you a family."

He grips my hair and yanks my head back. I cry out, but his other hands lifts, wrapping around my throat and cutting off my air.

I begin to panic and tear at his shirt. But he spins me around where my back is to his front, holding me in place. I gasp for a single breath but get nothing.

He lowers his lips to my ear. "You will give me as many children as I want. You were born to fucking breed, and that's exactly what you will do. You'll give me an army of men who I will train to run this world. Just as I was."

He shoves me forward, my heels getting caught in the netting of my dress, and I fall to the black rug. My fingers dig into the thick fibers as tears run down my face, and I choke out a sob. Turning, I look up at him. He's in the process of zipping up his pants when I manage to say, "I won't do it." I shake my head. "I won't allow you to do that to an innocent child." I scream the last part, but my voice breaks. "And a girl ..." I sob. Dear Lord, what if I have a girl? Would she see the same fate I have? I will never pack up her things and ship her off to live with a monster. Not as my mother did to me.

He smirks, reading my thoughts like they're written all

over my face. "You know my mother gave birth to a girl before me."

My eyes widen. "But ... you don't have any sisters."

"My father took her out back and threw her into the pool."

I gasp, my hand flying to my mouth. I wait for him to tell me that he's joking, but he doesn't. And deep down, I know it's true. Tears spill from my eyes, and my hatred for Mr. Bianchi grows. I always knew that man was sick. How could you hurt an innocent child?

"The word was my mom cried for days, weeks, even months after he killed her firstborn. I was born ten months later. Then she was gifted with Matteo. Then my twin brothers. But that wasn't enough. My father wanted one more son. Well, I was six when another girl came along. I stood outside their bedroom door and listened to the baby cry when she delivered. My mother instantly started bawling. She knew the child's fate would be the same as her first daughter. But she begged my father not to kill her." He kneels in front of me. "Do you know what she said?"

I just stare up at him through watery eyes.

"She said, 'Let me keep her. I'll train her to be a lady, so she can be useful to you as a woman.'"

My body begins to shake, and I swallow that knot that forms in my throat.

"You see, Haven, we all play a role in this life, and a woman is very useful if she knows her place." Then he stands, turns, and walks out of his office.

Leaving the threat hanging in the air.

LUCA

I WALK DOWN the hallway, nodding to guests and shaking hands with a smile on my face.

Fuck them all!

I invited them to show off my bride-to-be, so they can see how powerful I am with her. My father looks at my mother like she is nothing, a toy to use, and I don't want that with Haven. No matter how hard on her I am, or what I say to her, I want her to run this city with me. I want her to be the Mafia wife my father always wanted but never got, and I know she can do it. No matter how much she fights it right now, she will be the best damn thing I ever do.

Walking out onto the back terrace, I spot the Kings standing over by the pool.

"Nice party," Bones says, lifting his glass of champagne as I approach.

"Thanks for coming, Kings."

"I never pass up free booze," Titan replies. "Or a hot piece of ass," he adds, his eyes glued to a brunette walking by us. Without saying another word, he follows her.

"Grave? May I speak to you for a moment?" I ask.

He nods, stepping away from the guys, and we make our way over to the other end of the pool. The white lights floating on top of the calm water give off a soft glow along with the strand of white lights hung from one end of the patio to the other. I wanted to make this place as pretty as possible for Haven, but I don't even think she's been out here to see it.

"Did it work?" he asks immediately once we're out of earshot.

"Yep," I answer, sliding my hand into my pocket and pulling out a baggie. "Thanks for the help and make sure to share with Lucy."

He places it in his pocket and chuckles. "Anytime."

THE PARTY HAS STARTED TO DIE DOWN. CHECKING MY Rolex watch, I see it's a little after eleven p.m. I haven't seen Haven since she found me with my pants undone in my office. And no one has bothered to ask me where my future wife went. To most of these men, women are insignificant. To them, her absence is just her way of obeying my commands. As though I ordered her to go and wait naked in our bed until I was ready to fuck her.

"Nice play, Luca." My father slaps me on the back. He looks to the left as Bones walks past us. He smiles to himself, conjuring up a plan in his mind. He wants Kingdom, and he knows exactly what to do to get it. "I look forward to this business plan of yours." He's referring to my marriage. And I'll die before I allow him to fuck it up. "But I still think Maria would have been a nice fit to the Bianchi family."

I fist my hands at his words but give him a smile. I've been trained to stay silent when you don't agree with him. "Where is Mother?" I ask, changing the subject.

"She left earlier." He tips back his champagne flute and eyes one of the waitresses who works for the catering service I hired for the evening. She's currently talking to Titan who is eye fucking her. "Wasn't feeling well."

I bet she wasn't. She doesn't want me to marry Haven. She's disappointed in me and felt that such a sweet girl deserved better. I don't disagree with her.

"I got a call last night," he says. "Heard that Rossi's wedding chapel was hit. And Anthony is missing." Diaz's son.

Matteo snorts from beside him. "They won't find a body."

"I did what needed to be done," I offer.

I expect my father to argue, but instead, he just takes another drink.

"I'm off to bed," I tell him and turn to Nite who walks up next to us. "Kick everyone out and clean it all up," I order.

He gives me a curt nod.

I make my way upstairs to the master suite. I enter, not surprised when I don't see Haven in our bed. But she's mistaken if she thinks I'll let her ignore me tonight. I've allowed her to sleep downstairs for two nights now. That's more than enough.

I undo my tie and rip it out from the collar of my white button-down. Laying it over the chair that sits in front of the bay window, I undo my shirt and shove it off my shoulders and then head into our en suite bathroom.

Opening the door, I find her standing by the whirlpool tub in the corner of the bathroom. She lets out a growl as she tries to reach around and undo the zipper on her dress.

"Would you like some assistance?" I ask.

She spins around to face me. Her watery brown eyes narrow on me, but she says nothing.

"I've been looking for you." *Lie.*

"Get out," she orders, then goes back to trying to reach the zipper again.

"Let me help you." I walk across the bathroom, but she shoves me back when I get close.

"Don't fucking touch me!" she shouts, looking me up and down with disgust. "You think I'd let you come near me after you fucked that whore?"

She's drunk.

I know it. She knows it. I told her no alcohol, but I know she spent an hour down in the wine cellar. Nothing happens in this house that I'm not aware of. I could have stopped her, but I chose not to. A bottle of wine wasn't going to hurt her. And I needed the time to put my plan into action.

"Do you really think I fucked another woman in my office at our engagement party?"

"I know what I saw." She seethes, slapping me across the face before heading for the door. Stomping the heels of her Jimmy Choos so hard that I fear they may break.

"You saw what I wanted you to see," I say calmly, feeling my cheek throb from her hand. It wasn't as hard as it could have been. The alcohol's making her weaker, but I like the way it feels. It tells me that she cares.

She slowly turns to face me. She blinks. Once. Twice. I can see the words turning in her mind. The shock evident on her face. "No," she says roughly and shakes her head.

Fuck, I wanna bend her over the counter and fuck her from behind. It's been too long since I've had her. Felt her. Heard her scream my name. I want to remind her what I do to her. How I made her feel. We can get past this, if only she would let it go.

"I saw her ... the blonde, walk out of your office, then fix her hair and makeup. Then you came out of your bathroom with your pants unzipped." She swallows. "The used condom ... you even confessed you fucked her."

I shake my head. "I did no such thing."

"Luca ..."

"I made you believe that I fucked her because that's what I wanted you to think."

Her shoulders begin to shake. "Why?" she croaks out, and a tear runs down her face.

"For this reason, right here. To prove that you still love

me." I walk over to her, and she doesn't pull away when I reach up and cup her wet cheek.

"I don't love you," she whispers, biting her bottom lip.

"Lie," I say, dropping my hand lower to grip her hip. Deep down, she knows I'd never hurt her. Not like that. I have loved this woman for as long as I can remember. How can she think that would just go away? That I could ever walk away from her if it wasn't for a good reason? Haven isn't the kind of woman you forget. She's the kind you never stop thinking about. She's in your daily thoughts and even in your dreams.

She sniffs. "Why would you do this?"

I sigh. "I needed to know that what we have is real."

She shoves me away, her face growing hard. "This isn't fucking real. You're forcing me to marry you. And this fucking dress ..." She trails off, her hands trying to reach the zipper, but it's too high.

I spin her around, grip the expensive fabric, and rip it apart. The soft pink lace gives way along with the seam. She gasps as it falls to pool at her feet.

SEVEN

HAVEN

I STAND BEFORE him in a white lace thong and my pink high heels. That's it. The once expensive pink dress lies ripped on the marble floor of the bathroom. Just like my heart. He tricked me. He wanted me to think he cheated. Why? Because he wanted me to get jealous? Will this be my life from now on? Game after game? Test after test? I'll fail all of them.

He's right. I was jealous. But I can't forgive him for what he did. Or what he made me think he did.

My lips purse, and my hands fists. I lean into his face. "I will not play a role in your fucking life, Luca." Then I turn around and go to leave the bathroom.

His hand grips my hair and yanks me back. I cry out as he places me in front of the bathroom mirror, shoving my hips into the white and gray marble countertop. His hand stays in my hair while the other comes around and grips my chin.

"Luca, what are you—"

"Look at yourself," he interrupts me, shaking my chin. I

107

whimper. "Tell me I'm not the only one who has ever loved you."

I swallow the knot that instantly forms in my throat. My watery eyes meet his cold stare in the mirror, begging him to stop, pleading with him not to do this, but he shows no sign of mercy. "No ..."

He spins me around and cups my face. His dark eyes glare down at me. "Your biological mother didn't want you."

"Stop." My body shakes.

"Your adopted parents didn't want you." His voice rises.

"Please," I cry.

"They sold you into the Mafia, a world that they know you may not be able to survive, for five million dollars!" he screams.

"Stop!" I shout back.

"Where are they, Haven?" he demands, his hands gripping my upper arms painfully. "Where the fuck are the people who were supposed to love you?"

I punch his chest. My fists just slide off, and my body shakes. I hate that he's right. That he's all I have left. It wasn't supposed to be like this. My life. Our love. "You son of a bitch," I choke out. "I ... hate ... you ..."

"Quit lying," he growls. "Quit acting like this isn't what you've always wanted."

"You're not my savior," I cry, hating that he feels as though he's doing me a favor. As if he didn't love me, then no one else ever would.

He smirks. "You can't raise hell with a saint, darling."

"What is that supposed to mean?"

"It means you're no innocent, and I have a job to do," he growls.

"Now I'm a job?" I shout. "I thought you were doing me a favor?"

"What I'm doing is none of your business," he snaps.

"This is my life!" I seethe. "And I don't want you anywhere near it!"

He yanks me to him, and before I can even open my mouth to protest, he slams his lips to mine, aggressively kissing me. I open for him as I always have, and I hate that I pull him closer to me. That I need the contact. I need to feel something.

Luca has always been my home. My protector. But that changed when he left me alone. Vulnerable.

I pull back and slap him across the face. The sound bounces off the cream walls. "Fuck you."

Without missing a beat, he grips my thighs, lifts me up and slams my ass down onto the countertop. The cold surface makes me whimper.

He spreads my legs wide, coming to stand between them.

I try to shove him away, but he easily pushes my hands behind my back and holds them in place by my wrists. His lips fall to my neck. "Fight me, Haven," he growls, his teeth nipping at my sensitive skin, and goose bumps break out across my body. "Pretend you don't want me to fuck you."

"Luca ..." I breathe his name.

"Tell me you don't want this. That you don't want me." Taking both of my wrists in one of his hands, his now free hand grips my hair and yanks my head back.

The sound of heavy breathing fills the large bathroom. My chest rising and falling quickly. My nipples are hard, and my mouth is dry. Add the alcohol to my lack of sex life, and I'm completely fucked.

Letting go of my hair, he straightens and runs his hand up my rib cage and cups my breast. He licks his lips as his thumb runs over my pebbled nipple before pinching it.

I cry out, and he releases my wrists. My fingers run through his hair, my nails digging into his scalp. He hisses in a breath before ripping my underwear from my hips. The fabric cuts into my skin before giving in to his strength.

His hand falls between my parted legs, and he shoves a finger into my pussy.

I throw my head back and cry out.

"Tell me," he orders.

"What ...?" My breath gets caught in my throat as he adds another.

I could almost cry at the sensation that I've longed for so long. No memory or dream could come close to the real thing. To him.

"How many guys have you fucked since me, Haven?" he growls.

"Enough." I pant.

A growl rumbles his chest. His free hand comes up, grabs a handful of my hair, and yanks my head back again.

His dark eyes bore down on mine. And for once, I don't shrink back. I forget about why I'm here and the ripped dress that lies on the marble floor. My heart pounds and my pussy throbs. I'm wet for him.

I need to be reminded that I'm his.

It's pathetic and completely wrong, but that's us. Nothing about our lives has ever been clear. Or morally right.

I lick my parted lips, and whisper, "How many women have you fucked since me, Luca?" I shouldn't ask, but the alcohol makes me daring. Stupid even. Why not cut myself and bleed for him?

He gives me a smile that makes my heart beat faster. "You really wanna know, Haven?" he asks, running his nose long my jaw.

"Yes," I growl, trying to swallow. He still holds my neck back at an odd angle, and my pussy throbs, begging for his fingers to return.

"Five," he answers. His nose runs along my chin. "Each one better than the last."

I ball my fists and hit him in the arms.

"Get mad, baby," he whispers roughly. "Spread those soft legs and let me show you why you were always my favorite."

LUCA

ANOTHER LIE. I haven't been with anyone else since her. And it's going to stay that way.

She tries to push me away, but she's unsuccessful. Her hands slap at my chest, but then they fall to my slacks. She undoes them quickly and shoves them down my thighs, along with my boxers. She grips the base of my hard cock, and I jump when she squeezes it.

I grip her chin, forcing her to look up at me. When our eyes meet, we both freeze. We're both panting, my heart pounds and her beautiful amber eyes are swimming in tears. They look like honey.

"I hate you," she whispers.

I almost believe that leaving her was wrong, but it wasn't. I did what needed to be done. Someone else needed me more than she did, so I won't apologize for that.

My free hand runs along her smooth pussy, her wetness covering my fingers. "Then why are you wet?"

She whimpers, rocking her hips against my hand, wanting more.

I slide a finger into her, teasing her once again. "Tell me you want me to fuck you."

"No—"

"Beg me to fuck you," I interrupt her, leaning my face down to hers. My tongue darts out, running along her parted lips. I thrust a second finger into her, and she sucks in a ragged breath. Her legs tighten on my hips, pulling me closer to her. My cock is still in her hand, and she grips it like a vise. "Come on, Haven," I coo. "Use that pretty mouth and tell me what you want."

My fingers slide out of her and then back in, running my thumb over her clit. Her body jerks as she gasps. "Ffuucckk."

"That's right, baby." I smile, doing it again. More forcefully.

I add a third finger, and she releases my cock. Her hands come up to my shoulders, and she digs her nails into my skin. "Oh, God ..."

"Say it," I whisper as my eyes roam her face. Her eyes are closed, her lips parted, and her chest rising and falling fast. I wonder when a man last touched her. I know she was lying. I didn't find anything on her phone, but that doesn't mean she hasn't been seeing someone.

"Please," she begs. "Please fuck me."

Ripping her off the countertop, I carry her into the room. I throw her down onto the bed, her body bouncing a few times before I crawl on top of her. Spreading her legs with mine, I grip my cock and push into her, not waiting another second. I need her.

Her hands come up to my chest, but I pin them against the bed. She cries out as my hips begin to move. It's not slow. I'm not making love to her. I'm fucking her.

She arches her back, crying out, as I fucking take what I want.

She's never been able to tell me no, and I love that about

her. How much she needs me. Things aren't going to be any different than they were before, other than the fact we have a contract. One that states she can never leave me. Marriage into the Mafia is like being born into the Mafia. There is no escape other than death.

EIGHT

HAVEN

I OPEN MY eyes and roll over. A soft moan releases from my lips. I ache. Everywhere. It'd been too long, and I forgot how much stamina Luca had. He fucked me twice before I passed out. Then at one point, he woke me up, flipped me over, and took me from behind. I didn't protest one bit. If I remember correctly, I begged him then too.

I came all over his cock and sheets. I'm gonna pay for that today. Getting up, I grab a shirt that is thrown over a chair and slip it on. He tore my underwear off last night, and I haven't unpacked my stuff yet. Trying to be stubborn, I go without anything underneath. Thankfully, the shirt is long enough that it comes down close to my knees. I make my way down the stairs, listening for any voices. I'm not sure of his work schedule or if he is even still here. When my bare feet hit the landing, I see two men standing by the front door in the foyer, but they pay me no attention. And I hate how my stomach tightens at the thought of him needing this much security. It was never like this when he was in school. Or maybe I just didn't see it.

"Is Luca here?" I ask them, holding my shirt down my legs.

Nothing. No side-eye. No go fuck yourself. Just silence.

"Thanks," I mumble and walk down the hall. I'm about to go outside to see if his car is here when I hear voices coming from his office. The same one where I thought he fucked the blonde. Taking a deep breath, I square my shoulders and open the door.

I pause the moment I step inside. Luca sits behind his desk in a three-piece suit, his arms folded over his chest. And Bones is pacing back and forth.

"This is—"

"Haven," Luca interrupts him, and Bones comes to a stop. His head snaps up, and his eyes narrow on me.

I know Luca did that so I wouldn't get any information on their conversation, and it pisses me off.

"What are you doing in here?" he asks with a growl.

It's the same question he asked me last night when he found me at his desk. As if I'm not allowed. Like it's forbidden.

Ignoring him, I look at Bones, and he's glaring down at me. He's changed so much since college. He didn't have any tattoos back then, and now he's covered in them. Well, that's not true. I did see a tattoo on him. Once.

I STUMBLE DOWN THE HALLWAY, MY ARM LOCKED WITH Emilee's. She laughs as her Sprite and vodka spills over the rim of her cup. "Where is ... Jasmine?" She hiccups.

Placing my free hand on the wall to help guide us, I answer. "She's with Trenton."

She snorts loudly. "Thought we hated him."

"We did. Yesterday. He apologized to her after we

slashed his tires." I laugh, entering the living room and looking around aimlessly. "Where are the guys?"

It's Saturday night. The boys had a baseball game today. They won, like always, and they decided to throw a party to celebrate at Bones and Grave's father's house. Even for the place being a mansion, it's crowded with kids from the college.

"I was standing in the kitchen when Luca came and got Bones." She hiccups again. "Think he took him to the game room."

I reach over, take her drink from her hand, and down it. Only a few drops hit my shirt. "Let's go look."

It takes us longer than usual to make our way up the staircase and down the long hall that leads to the game room at the end.

I turn the knob and shove it open. We both go stumbling into the room. She giggles, and I say a few choice curse words, trying to get my sluggish legs to keep myself standing. Looking up, I see Bones leaning back against the pool table, his arms crossed over his chest. Luca stands before him, his hands in the front pockets of his dark-fitted jeans.

Our abrupt entrance catches their attention, and whatever they were discussing comes to an end.

"What are you guys doing up here?" I ask, shutting the door with my foot and untangling my arm from Emilee.

"Talking business," Bones's answer is clipped as his eyes move from mine to hers.

I frown. "Business?"

"Well, now it's time to party," Emilee says, stumbling over to him like Bambi. He uncrosses his arms and catches her as she falls against his chest.

"Wanna party, do you?" he asks, looking down at her, a smile tugging at the corner of his lips.

Luca comes to stand behind me and wraps his arms around my waist. I lean into him, letting him support my drunk ass.

"Yep." She giggles, reaching down and grabbing the hem of her shirt. She lifts it up and over her head.

Ohhh.

I watch with complete fascination, staring at my best friend. Her long dark hair lifts with the fabric before falling to cover her back.

His eyes drop to her chest, and his hands grip her hips. "We'll have an audience, Em."

Reaching behind her, she undoes her bra before removing the straps from each shoulder. "Wouldn't be the first time, would it?"

My body heats up at the thought. Luca and I aren't shy in the bedroom, but no one has ever watched us. And we've never watched someone else before either. Not besides a few porn videos.

He arches a brow, just realizing something that they both already knew, but says, "No. It wouldn't be."

Luca's right hand comes up and pulls my hair back, exposing my bare shoulder to him since I'm in a tube top. My breath hitches when I feel his lips on my bare skin.

"Are you gonna stop me?" she asks him, lowering her hands to the button on his jeans.

"No," he answers roughly.

She undoes the second button, then the third. She goes down to her knees, yanking his jeans down his thighs. He wasn't wearing anything underneath them. I know I shouldn't look at him, not with Luca standing behind me, but he's not stopping me. He's not pulling me away. Instead, he tangles his hand in my hair and gently tugs my head to the side as his lips trail up and down my neck.

I pant as Emilee reaches up and takes Bones's long and hard dick in her hand and begins to stroke it.

Luca's lips trail over my collarbone and up my neck once again. "Oh, God," I whimper, my legs tightening.

Bones and Emilee ignore us as he slides his hands into her long dark hair. His blue eyes so dark they look almost black as he stares down at her. I've never seen Bones in action, but I've heard about their sex life. I never understood her need to crawl to him whenever he called, but I see it right now. The way he looks at her like she rules his fucking world. She may be the one on her knees, but she's the one in charge.

"Suck my cock, Em. Show them how good you are at being dirty," he orders her.

Luca's hand slides down my waist and undoes my shorts. My breath hitches when he pushes the zipper down.

I should look away, but I can't. My eyes are glued to Emilee on her knees with Bones's cock in her hands. Opening her mouth, she licks up his shaft, twirling her tongue around the tip before closing her lips over it.

Bones stares down at her. His tongue comes out and runs across his lips slowly.

"Watch her please him, baby," Luca whispers in my ear. "'Cause you're up next." He presses his hips into my ass, and I feel his hard dick.

My heart pounds in my chest as he pushes my shorts down my legs. "Oh, God," I whimper when he pulls my thong to the side and runs his finger over my pussy.

Emilee picks up her pace. Her head bobs back and forth as Bones begins to fuck her mouth harder. His hands still fist her hair, and he watches his cock slide in and out, biting his bottom lip. His biceps straining against his shirt. He lets out a moan at her performance.

My pussy tightens when Luca's finger enters me. And I hitch in a breath when he shoves a second one in roughly.

"Do you like watching him use her?" Luca whispers hoarsely in my ear.

I nod, unable to speak.

He chuckles. "You're so wet, Haven. Watching your best friend on her knees while I finger you turns you on."

I moan when he rubs my clit with his thumb.

Emilee whimpers as Bones violently fucks her mouth. His hips slam into her, and I'm jealous. Not of him. But of her. I wanna please Luca the way she's pleasing Bones. It turns me on to know that I can be that girl for him.

"Fuck, you're good, Em." Bones moans, throwing his head back, his Adam's apple bobbing while he swallows. "Fuck, yeah. That's it."

Her hands grip his naked and toned thighs, and her hair bounces off her bare back.

I cry out when Luca enters a third finger into me.

"Shh." He slaps his free hand over my mouth, silencing me, still holding my back to his front. "You'll get your chance to be the center of attention," he growls before biting my neck. A shiver runs through me.

Bones thrusts forward one last time before he lets out a moan, holding her head in place as he comes in her mouth, forcing her to swallow. He pulls out of her lips, and a trail of cum runs down her chin.

He doesn't let her recover. He yanks her to her feet, then pulls her over to the couch that sits along the back wall. Sitting down, he spins her around to face us, then pulls her onto his lap. She straddles him backward, her knees up on the couch, her legs spread wide. Her once perfect makeup leaves black streaks down her face from his force. Her watery eyes are heavy, and she's panting. He reaches his hands around her body. One goes to her breast, the other yanks her mini skirt up around her waist. He slides his hand into her red panties, and she whimpers. The wet spot evidence of her arousal.

And I understand why she so willingly drops anything for him at any given time. He just fucked her mouth, and she looks like she came.

He leans forward, whispering something in her ear. Her heavy eyes meet mine, and she licks her already wet lips.

My thighs clench. Luca removes his fingers from inside me, and I sag against him at the loss.

"You're up," he whispers, slapping me on the ass. "Lie on the floor."

I comply without argument. Lying flat on my back, I look up at the ceiling, the room spinning. It reminds me of the Tilt-a-Whirl at the fair, and I pray that I don't get sick. I should have never drank as much as I did.

Luca comes to stand next to me. He unzips his jeans and then pulls his impressively large and very hard cock through the hole in his black boxers. I lick my lips. He falls to his knees, straddling me, and I reach out to grab his dick in my hands, but he grips my wrists, stopping me.

I whimper and lift my hips.

"You know how I like it." Scooting up, he straddles my face. He crosses my wrists above my head, pinning them to the soft rug in one hand and grabs the base of his cock with his free hand. And I open for him.

He runs the tip of his dick over my lips, and I feel the precum cover them. My tongue darts out and licks up his shaft before he presses into me.

I moan as he fills my mouth. My hips buck empty air, wishing his mouth was between my legs. I love sixty-nine.

I hear Emilee moan in the distance, but I don't dare look

away from Luca's face hovering above me. His eyes are glued to mine. His lips are parted, and his breathing has picked up. I tilt my head back a little more, and his hips pick up. My nipples are hard, my pussy soaked, and I lie here while he fucks my mouth.

He hits the back of my throat, and tears sting my eyes. He doesn't let up; if anything, he goes harder, faster. Like he always does. How I like it.

He hovers over me with a look of determination on his face and lust in his eyes. I'm turned on, and it's turning him on.

He shoves to the back of my throat, and I force myself to swallow.

"Fuck," he growls. "That's what I like."

I do it again.

"Goddamn, Haven."

Tears spill down the sides of my face, and my mouth screams from being open so wide, but he doesn't stop.

His body straddles my chest. Finding it hard to breathe through my nose,

I feel the room spin faster. My vision going blurry.

He thrusts harder, faster, and his hands tighten on my wrists. I know they'll be bruised tomorrow.

I don't give two shits.

Suddenly, he pulls out, and I suck in a breath, my chest heaving.

He rips my thong down my legs, and I almost cry in relief.

Then grabbing my arm, he yanks me up and onto all fours. Lifting my heavy head, I look up to see Emilee completely naked now, straddling Bones facing us while he still lounges behind her on the couch. His hands grip her narrow hips as she rides him. Her hair sticks to her slick face and chest. I watch shamelessly as she bounces on his cock. Her cum dripping down his balls and onto the leather couch.

"Spread your legs," Luca orders before he slaps me on the ass.

I whimper but do as he says.

He comes up behind me. He shoves two fingers into my soaked pussy, and I cry out. Then he pulls them out just as quickly and replaces them with his cock. He grips a handful of hair and yanks my head back. "Watch him fuck her while I fuck you." His legs spread mine farther apart, making my thighs burn.

Emilee reaches up and grabs her breasts, her lips parting. Bones releases her hips and pulls her arms back, sliding his forearm between them and her back to lock her arms in place. His free hand comes up and wraps around her throat, pulling her head back. I hear her take in a strangled breath. Her tits bounce, her hair covers half her face. I watch her body tense and her lips part before she's coming all over him again.

"That's it, Em. How many times will you come for me tonight?" he growls, not letting up.

I look at him. Bones no longer wears a shirt, and I catch sight of a tattoo on his chiseled chest. A crown hangs off the side of a skull. A set of crossbones below it. And I know it stands for Kings.

The Dark Kings.

"Haven?"

I jump back at the sound of my name. My head whips to look at Luca. His eyes narrow on me, and I feel my face heat with embarrassment. Was I just checking out Bones? Fuck, I hope I didn't say anything. Or moan at the memory.

Shit!

I clench my thighs because I didn't put any underwear on, and now my pussy is wet.

"Will you give me and my *fiancée* a minute?" Luca asks tightly.

My heart flutters at him calling me that. It's the first time he's said it out loud.

Bones doesn't say anything, but his shoulder brushes mine as he walks out and slams the door shut. I flinch at the sound.

"Luca—"

"I was in the middle of a meeting," he interrupts me. "What is it that you need?"

My hands fist. "I wanted to ..." I pause because I'm not sure what I wanted. Did I expect him to love me after last night? Did I expect him to bring me breakfast in bed? Or whisk me away on a plane to a private island? I'm not sure what I thought.

"Nothing," I settle on, not sure what to say. Now ashamed.

He stands, buttoning his suit jacket, and then walks around his desk. I go to leave, but he reaches out and grabs my upper arm, pulling me into him.

"Luca ..."

"Do you need me to fuck you?" he asks, cupping my face. "Is that why you came barging in here?" His eyes roam my disheveled hair and the oversized T-shirt I wear. I didn't know there would always be so many people here at the house. Now I know to always be covered up when I leave the bedroom.

"No."

He cocks an eyebrow. "Are you sure? Because you were looking at Bones like you were in the mood for dick."

I swallow nervously and look away from him.

He grips my chin and forces my attention back up at him. "Is that what you want, Haven?" He lets go of my chin and trails his knuckles down my neck. "Want me to call Bones back in here so he can bend you over the desk and fuck you?"

My eyes narrow up at him, and my chest tightens.

His eyes darken. "Or maybe I should call him back in here so he can watch *me* fuck you."

"Fuck you, Luca!" I shout, slamming my fists into his chest.

He grips my wrist and places my hand to his slacks. He's hard, and my already wet pussy tightens. "Hmm?" he asks. "Were you remembering the time we watched him fuck Emilee?"

"Luca ..." His name is whispered, and a slow smile spreads across his face. If he was guessing, he just got his answer.

He reaches down and raises the hem of his shirt that I wear. His brows rise when he sees I'm not wearing anything underneath. I close my eyes in embarrassment.

"You were thinking of him and her."

"Luca ...?"

"As much fun as that was, I want you to know that will never happen again, Haven," he growls.

I nod.

"You belong to me. And I won't share you. Do you understand?"

"Yes," I whimper.

"Not with him. Not with anyone. I will be the only one to see you come. To see my cock in your mouth. Or in your pussy."

"Please," I beg, not sure what I'm begging for.

"You need me, baby? Is that why you barged in here?"

125

He doesn't wait for me to answer. He grips the back of my neck and shoves me over the desk. I breathe onto the surface as I hear him unzip his pants. He fucks me, violently. He doesn't cover my mouth as I scream out his name, and I know he did it on purpose. He wanted the house to hear him dominate me. And I was one hundred percent okay with it.

LUCA

HAVEN EXITS MY office as Bones re-enters. He sits down in the seat across from my desk and crosses his arms over his chest.

My office now smells of sex, and I'm still hard. I could totally go another round, but I have work to do. I have a feeling I won't get shit done now that she's living here with me.

"You were saying?" I clear my throat.

"Word on the street is that retaliation is coming your way."

This is why we intertwine our lives and business with the Kings. They have eyes and ears everywhere. They reach places we can't.

I lean back in my chair. "We knew it would happen." You don't slaughter six men and expect to get away with it. It's taken time for them to rebuild their army, and I took out their frontline. Leaving their dismembered bodies behind didn't sit well with them. "They have sat on their asses long enough. I figured our appearance at the wedding chapel would get our message across."

He nods, and his eyes slide to the closed door before they return to me.

"What?" I ask.

"Haven."

"What about her?" I ask, sitting up straighter. Was he daydreaming about me fucking her too? That was all fun and games when we were younger, but I was telling her the truth when I said it wouldn't ever happen again.

He leans forward, placing his tatted arms on the surface of my desk. "My father always says, 'Show me a man in love, and I'll show you his greatest weakness.'"

I tilt my head to the side. "You think they'll go for her?" It's not unrealistic.

"You did just announce your engagement. It's all over the papers and on social media." He sits back. "It's exactly what I would do. A woman is helpless compared to a man. Especially one with no training."

"I have guards on her." Rossi will never get the opportunity to touch her.

He arches a brow. "Are they enough?"

I slam my fists down on the desk, not happy about him second-guessing me. "Of course."

"Enough to bet her life on?" He goes on.

"Bones!"

He shrugs. Bones doesn't give a fuck. He has a careless attitude. Only three people matter to him and that's the Kings. And his Kingdom. Anyone else is fair game, women included. As he said, they are easy targets.

"I'm just asking if there are holes where someone could slip through."

I run a hand through my hair. "Nite is covering it."

He nods. "Then I guess we're done here." He stands and walks over to the door.

"Bones?" I ask, and he pauses, turning to face me. "Set me up a meeting with Titan later on today," I order.

"I'll have him call you." Then he exits the room, leaving the door open.

Nite enters immediately, and I look up at him. He stands before my desk, dressed in black dress pants and a white button-down. His shoulder holster has a gun on each side. I don't doubt his loyalty. He's proven it to this family once before.

WE ENTER THE CABIN, AND A MAN LIES ON THE FLOOR IN the living room. His right hand grips his bloody left arm. A snake had bit him. He's also bleeding from his right thigh. And a snake is still wrapped around his left ankle.

I remove my gun from my holster and shoot the snake, the bullet going right through his ankle. He screams out, his body jerking.

I reach down, grab the snake, and toss it to the corner of the room.

He looks up at me through watery eyes. He takes in my clothes, and how they are covered in Bernard's blood. "You'll pay for this."

"Funny, that's exactly what Bernard said."

"Fucking pay!" he shouts. "They'll find her."

My hand tightens on the gun.

"They will fucking send her back to you in pieces!" he screams. "When they're done with her, you won't even have a body to identify." He sucks in a breath through his teeth.

My jaw clenches, and my muscles tighten. No! They will not! I won't let them.

He smiles up at me. "That's after they use her, of course."

My body begins to shake with pure anger. My muscles tight, and my mind seeing a hundred different scenarios of her bloody and dead.

"Don't worry, they'll make sure to give her exactly what you deserve."

I drop to my knees and wrap my hand around his throat. "They'll never touch her," I growl.

Nite makes his way up the old wooden stairs and tosses a rope over the banister before tying it off. I wrap it around the guy's wrists and stand. Nite pulls the rope tight, hauling him up. He dangles in his restraints, fighting for leverage with his feet, but he can't get it. They're no longer touching the floor.

I remove my knife from my boot and flip open the blade.

"I've seen it before." He smiles at me, enjoying the fact that he's getting to me. "The way they use them. The way they torture them. She'll be the perfect revenge on the Bianchi family." He leans his head back to look up at Nite who still stands upstairs. "You should have just given her up."

I look up at the man I consider my brother. We haven't spoken about what exactly happened when they removed his tongue seven days ago. He was dumped on the doorstep with a note that said forever silent. *We knew he had been taken. For the three days he was missing, I was skipping my classes to look for him. And honestly, we never expected to find his body. But instead of death, they wanted him to suffer by never talking again. To know what it's like not to be able to speak for yourself and only take orders.*

I thought he protected my father. Our family. But he protected one person, in particular. And at this very moment, I realize that I can never repay him. No matter how many guys I kill for him, it'll never be enough.

No one talks about her. No one mentions her. We keep her hidden so she remains untouchable. "I'm going to gut you like a fish and leave you here to rot," I say to him.

He laughs like I'm fucking funny. "Go ahead and do

your worst, you sorry son of a bitch. Whatever you do to me, they will make sure to do to her."

"Over my dead body," I growl.

He throws his head back, this time his bloody body shaking with his laughter. "After you see what they do to her, you'll wish they would have just killed you."

THAT WAS FOUR YEARS AGO.

Now the time has come, and we need to be ready. I look up at my best friend. "Pack a bag. We're leaving."

A look of dread washes over his face before he masks it and nods before exiting my office.

I stand, place my hands on my desk and close my eyes. I will not allow anyone to touch her. As long as I'm alive, I will protect her with my life. "Goddammit!" I shout.

NINE

HAVEN

I EXIT THE shower and hear him enter the bedroom. After wrapping the towel under my arms, I step into the bedroom.

"Are your bags still packed?" Luca asks, storming to his closet.

"Yes," I answer, following him.

"Where are they?" he demands.

"In my closet," I say, entering his. He's throwing shit into a suitcase. "What's going on?"

"Here." He reaches into his pocket and tosses me my phone. I catch it in the air. "Get dressed. We're leaving in twenty."

Leaving? "Where are we going?" I ask.

"To Kingdom." Then he storms out of his closet and into mine. I run after him. He grabs a couple of my bags and sets them in the middle of the bedroom.

I frown. "Why do I need bags to go to Kingdom?" I ask confused. "Are we staying there?"

"No," he snaps as his cell begins to ring. He looks down

at it and hits answer. "Titan ..." He pauses, then exits the room, shutting the door behind him.

I look down at my phone in my hand. He hasn't been charging it, so the battery shows eight percent. Biting my bottom lip, I go to my call log and pull up Jasmine's number. Before I can second-guess what is happening, I press call.

She picks up on the third ring. "What up, ho?"

"I don't have much time," I say in greeting. Staring at the closed bedroom door, I wait for Luca to return. He wouldn't have given me my phone back if I wasn't allowed to use it, right? "Whatever you're doing, stop. And meet me at Kingdom in twenty minutes."

<hr />

I SIT INSIDE EMPIRE, THE STEAKHOUSE THAT SITS ON the twentieth floor of Kingdom. My knees bounce, and I chew on my bottom lip nervously. I have no clue what is going on. I hurried to get ready after Jasmine agreed to meet me. And when Luca returned to the bedroom, he was off the phone and telling me it was time to go. Nite brought us here. But the moment we arrived, Luca told me to mind Nite and left me. Just as I had hoped he would. For some reason, I knew we were coming here for him to meet Titan. And Luca wasn't going to allow me to be involved in whatever they wanted to discuss. I figured that out earlier in his office when he was having a meeting with Bones. He may be forcing me to marry him, but he wants to keep me in the dark when it comes to business. A part of me is okay with that because nothing involving the Dark Kings is good.

I look up from the booth and see Jasmine enter. I jump up and run to her. She wraps her arms around me and picks me up off my feet like she hasn't seen me in years.

"Oh my God," she shrieks, putting me down. She looks the same as she did when I saw her a few weeks ago. She's been dying her hair red for the past couple of years. She wears it up in a high ponytail today with a Neffex T-shirt on and holey jeans with a pair of Converse. You wouldn't think her dad is a millionaire. I've always loved that about her.

We sit down, and her eyes slide over to the entrance. "Is that Oliver Nite?"

I sigh. "Yeah. He's my babysitter."

She lifts her chin to him. "Hey, Nite?" she calls out. "Do you charge by the hour? How much for an overnight?"

"Jasmine ..."

"I'm serious." She whistles looking him up and down. "Damn, he's hotter than he was in college."

He doesn't acknowledge her in any way. With his arms crossed over his chest, he stares straight ahead.

She laughs, giving me her attention. "I'm pretty sure he's gay."

"What? No ..."

"Yep." She nods. "You never saw him with a girl back in school. Never heard of him with a woman. Then he took that vow of silence." She looks back over at him. "You can be my bitch, Nite. If that's what you're into."

I choke on air as his eyes slam to hers at her words. She blows him a kiss. "I have a strap-on. No judgement." She throws her hands up in the air. "I've experimented with girls before. I know how to use it."

He looks at her like he's about to body slam her ass into the ground. And not in a good way.

I run a hand down my face. "When was the last time you got laid?"

"Well, my hoodie got caught on the doorknob as I was leaving the house yesterday and the collar choked me. My nipples got hard and my cunt wet. It was the most action I've had in three weeks."

Same ole Jasmine. I smile at her. I miss her. I miss both my best friends. "Have you spoken to Emilee lately?"

"She was in town a couple of weeks ago."

I look down at my cell that sits on the table. It has officially died. "What? She didn't tell me."

She nods. "I gave her a call, and she sounded out of breath. I asked her if she was fucking. She went silent for a second and then explained she was boarding a plane back to Chicago."

I sit back in the booth. "Why didn't she call and tell me?"

"She was just in town for the day. It's her mom ... She's sick."

My chest tightens. "Sick how?"

"Lymphoma. Stage four."

I gasp.

"Gave her six months to live. She was heading back to Chicago to pack up her things and place her apartment on the market so she can move back here and help her father take care of her."

"Why ...?" I swallow. Gripping my phone, I wish I could call her and tell her I'm sorry. That I love her, and that I'm here for her. "Why hasn't she told me this?"

She shrugs. "You know how Emilee deals with things. I've tried calling her since, but she never answers."

"How did we get here?" I ask.

"Celibate?"

It makes me laugh at how she deflects. "No. So distant. We used to be inseparable."

She shrugs again. "Life happens. We get older, and everything goes to shit." She reaches for a piece of calamari off the plate I ordered in the middle of the table and shoves it in her mouth. "You should see my tits. Time has not been nice to them."

I doubt that. They're fake. But instead of reminding her of that, I say, "I'm getting married."

She looks up at me through her dark lashes. Her hands pause with more calamari. "My hearing must be going to shit as well 'cause it sounded like you just said you're getting married."

I hold up my left hand to show her my ring.

Her eyes widen. "You're gonna be a ..."

"Bianchi," I finish for her.

Sitting back in her seat she releases a heavy sigh. "What? How ...? When did you get back together?"

Tears sting my eyes, and I lick my lips. Taking in a deep breath, I fill her in.

***

"Say something," I prompt, hating sitting here in silence.

She blinks. "I ... uh ..." Clearing her throat, she shifts in her seat. "What's the problem here?"

"Jasmine," I growl.

"What? Haven." She reaches across the table and grabs my hand. "I honestly don't see the issue. You love Luca. You've always loved him. Now he's all yours."

I remove my hand from hers. "Only on paper."

"You don't know that. Have you given him a chance? Sat down and really spoken to him?"

My mouth falls open. "Unbelievable."

"Haven ..."

135

"You're supposed to be on my side. He slept with another woman."

"Made you think he slept with another woman," she corrects me. "This is all you've ever wanted. Why are you fighting it so much?"

"Because he didn't want me," I say softly. "It's all about money. Power."

"I don't believe that for a second." She shakes her head. "I think you're just afraid."

"Am not."

"You're afraid that for once in your life, it's not falling apart."

I roll my eyes.

"Look at you." She gestures to me. "You've been a total mess since he left for Italy. You spent most of your time in a bottle of wine or drowning in a tub of ice cream. Your life is a mess ..."

"Thank you." I snort. "We both know that yours is just perfect."

She tilts her head to the side. "I'm not about to say I have my shit together. But we both know this isn't about me." She looks down at her hands knotted on the table. "I have my own issues when it comes to love, and I know that if I was offered the same opportunity as you, I'd jump on it without thought. Even if it came with a contract and a payment."

She's referring to Trenton. After all these years, she's still hung up on him. Even though the guy is now married.

Her eyes meet mine. "Just give him a chance. Maybe it'll turn out to be the best thing to ever happen to you."

"Or the worst," I add.

I feel a set of eyes on me. I look up, and Luca is standing

beside Nite. His eyes on mine as he speaks to him. And I know my time with my friend is over.

LUCA

AN HOUR LATER, we're boarding my private jet. Nite sits down across from me, and Haven sits to my right. Two men by the name of Max and Gabe sit on either side of Nite.

Titan gave them to me. He said that they are the best he has, and he trusts them with everything. So I told them to pack their shit, they were going on a trip. This is their training. Maybe I'll bring them back alive, maybe I won't. That depends on them.

Haven pulls her shade down and cuddles up with her pillow. Closing her eyes, I watch her breathing even out as she falls into a deep sleep.

Nite gets my attention when he runs a hand through his hair. He looks nervous.

"So when are we going to be informed of where we're going?" Max asks.

I'm not all that fond of them, but as long as they take orders, I won't slit their necks.

"Italy," I answer.

"For how long?" the other asks.

"We'll only be going for a couple of days." I look at Nite, and he swallows. He'll be staying behind.

TEN

HAVEN

HIRTEEN HOURS AND three naps later, our plane touches down in Sicily, Italy, where two cars await us outside of an airplane hangar. Luca ushers me into the back seat of the first one along with one of the guys I know to be named Max. Nite and the other guy climb into the second car. I stay silent, looking out the window of the car. I've been to Italy before. When I was nine, my parents brought me to the largest Mediterranean island for vacation. We stayed for a week, and I would move here in a heartbeat.

We pull up to a gate, but it opens before the car even rolls to a stop. I sit up straighter, watching as the grand Italian Palazzo-style mansion comes into view. The sun is starting to set in the background, making the illuminated structure look picture perfect. The car comes to a stop on the red brick driveway. The driver gets out, opening my door, and I exit, looking up at it in awe.

"Is this your place?" I ask Luca, not bothering to look over at him.

"No," he answers, taking my hand and leading me up the stone steps past the concrete columns.

Two wooden doors open, and we step inside. I look around, amazed at the expensive artwork hanging from the walls. And the detail work in the ceiling and floors.

"Where is she?" Luca asks a man who walks up to us.

I tense. *She?* In the past thirteen hours, I never once asked why we were coming here. My head whips to look over at him.

The man answers in Italian, and my lips thin.

Luca nods and then begins to drag me through the house until we're walking out an open glass door. And a woman stands in front of the Olympic-size infinity pool. The house sits on the side of a cliff, giving an ocean view. But all I can look at is the woman who has her back to us. She's got long lean legs. She wears a one-piece black bathing suit that is cut high on her narrow hips, showing off her bubble ass. Her long, thick dark hair tapers down to a V on her lower back. She wears a massive white hat that you would see at the Kentucky Derby. A black ribbon wrapped around the base is tied into a big bow on the side, and the ribbon hangs off the edge.

Luca says something in Italian, and again, I kick myself for not knowing the language.

The woman spins around, and her pouty red painted lips part on a gasp. She runs to him, throwing her arms around his neck.

He hugs her tightly. I'm instantly jealous. If he brought me here to meet his summer fling, I'm going to be pissed. Placing her down on her black wedges, she turns to face me. A pair of black Gucci glasses sits on her flawless Barbie face. My eyes roam over her small chest and tiny frame. She looks like a model who deserves to be on the cover of *Vogue*. I never look this good sitting by the pool. I never look this good at all actually.

"You must be Haven." She reaches her right hand out to me. Her English just as perfect as her Italian sounded. Just like her.

"I'm his fiancée," I correct her, lifting my chin. I instantly want to crawl under the table that sits to the right of me. I shouldn't show any kind of jealousy toward her because it just proves Luca right.

She giggles, and Luca gives a small cough.

"Congratulations." She gives me a big smile, showing off her dazzling smile. Teeth as white as fresh snow. They're also as straight as an arrow.

Fuck, is there anything wrong with this girl? She doesn't seem to have a single flaw. As if she's been groomed to bring any man to his knees.

"Haven ..." He throws his arm over her shoulders, pulling her into his side. "This is Mia Bianchi. My sister."

Uh ... "Your what?" *His sister?*

I was six when another girl came along. My mother instantly started bawling. She knew the child's fate would be the same as her first daughter. But she begged my father not to kill her. He had never said anything beyond that. I figured his dad had killed her as well. "But ...?"

She hugs me, pushing me back a little at her force. Giggling like a teenager, she whispers in my ear, "I've always wanted a sister."

I pat her back awkwardly as I try to wrap my head around this new information.

I look at him wide-eyed. Years together and he never once mentioned he had a sister. "Why would you keep this from me?"

"It's complicated," he answers tightly.

I snort, now pissed off for a different reason. "Complicated? Nothing about having a sister is complicated, Luca."

Mia smiles. "I like her."

Luca ignores her and steps into me. His jaw set in a hard line. "I don't expect you to understand."

"Try me," I challenge, looking back at his ... sister. She's smiling at me. *His fucking sister!* My eyes go back to his.

He opens his mouth, but one of my new bodyguards interrupts him. "Luca?"

"What?" he snaps at him.

"The perimeter is clear."

Luca steps away from me, turning and walking over to the guy before they walk away together.

"I'm sorry ..." Her pretty face falls. "I ..."

"It's not your fault," I tell Mia.

She's been hidden, kept a secret for how long? Luca said she was born six years after him, and I'm two years younger than him so that would make her twenty? Possibly twenty-one? "How long have you lived here?"

"Since I was thirteen," she answers.

I sigh, running a hand through my hair. "I ... I'm trying to wrap my head around this."

"Here." She grabs my hand and walks me over to a lounge chair by the pool. I plop down like a pig falling into mud while she sits on the one next to me with the grace of a fucking queen and crosses her right leg over her left.

Removing her hat, she pushes her glasses on the top of her head. My breath gets caught in my lungs when my eyes meet hers. They're the same silvery blue as their mother's. They make her look exotic with her tan skin and dark hair. She looks so much like their mother, it's scary.

"What do you want to know?" she asks me.

I blink, trying to wrap my head around what is happening. And how open she is going to be about it. "Luca hasn't told me a single thing regarding you." Well, that's a lie. *I heard about how your mother begged to keep you.* I don't think shipping her only daughter away was her wish.

"Not surprised."

"Why aren't you in Vegas?" I ask the first thing that comes to my mind.

"My father shipped me here on my thirteenth birthday because he didn't want anyone to know about me."

"But why?" I ask confused. Why does she have to be a secret?

"The Mafia life is a dark one. I know what my father and brothers do. And who they go after. Luca actually talked our father into sending me here."

My jaw tightens. "Luca is the reason you were exiled?"

She gives a soft chuckle. "It was best for me. To keep me safe."

I run a hand through my hair. "Are you really in that much danger?" The guys don't live here. Well, the twins have been gone for years, but I never really cared to ask where they were or why. Do they stay here with her? Were they shipped off as well?

She looks over at something, and I see Nite walk by us. She averts her eyes and inspects her red painted nails. "I was responsible for hurting him."

"Hurting him?" I ask, confused even more. "Hurting who? Luca?"

"Nite."

My brows pull together. She isn't making any sense. "How did you hurt him?"

Her silver eyes meet mine, and she tilts her head to the side. "He hasn't told you."

I shake my head. "No one has told me anything." I don't

know if she is referring to Luca or Nite. But I'm pretty sure everyone is aware that Nite hasn't spoken since their senior year in college.

"Have you heard of Alberto Rossi?" she asks.

I nod my head. "Yes."

She sighs. "He's my father's biggest rival in Vegas. It's been an ongoing fight for years. But they were once friends. Somehow, word got out that Rossi wanted me. He knew my father and brothers wouldn't give me up, not if they went to such great lengths to keep me hidden all that time, so he thought he'd be able to buy off a member of my father's crew."

"Who?"

"Oliver Nite."

I don't like where this is going.

"He was approached, and I'm not sure of those details, but whatever he said or did didn't sit well with Rossi. And for some reason, they thought they could get it another way. A week later, Oliver Nite was taken from his house. He had gone missing."

I remember when he missed school for a few weeks. When he came back, he never spoke again.

She looks down at her shoes and softens her voice. "He was tortured." My chest tightens. "They wanted intel on me, and he refused to give it. His loyalty to my family didn't waver." She shakes her head as if keeping her a secret was the stupidest thing he could have ever done. "They cut out his tongue for it." I gasp, and my hand comes up to cup my mouth. "They dropped him off at Luca's front door. A week later, Nite, Luca, and one of my father's men went after Rossi. Although he was not found, they did brutally slaughter six of his men in retaliation for what they did to Nite."

My head spins, but it all makes sense now. Why he doesn't talk. The vow of silence. It was a lie. "I didn't know ..."

"No one does. If it got out what happened to him, then my secret would be blown."

"But ... I don't understand. Why keep you a secret?"

Her silver eyes meet mine. "Because a player never shows his cards."

My chest tightens. Mr. Bianchi is going to use his daughter. He has a plan for her. He saved her by sending her here, but what kind of danger does her future hold? What could he possibly do with her?

I look over at Nite, who now stands by the pool with his arms crossed over his chest and a pair of Aviators on his face even though the sun has almost set. I see him in a different light now. We were never friends, but I never disliked him. I can't imagine what he went through and what kind of guilt Mia holds, knowing what happened to him.

"With Luca being here, that can only mean one thing." She sighs.

My head snaps back to hers. "What?" My heart picks up at her words because until now, I didn't know why the hell we were here.

"They're coming for me."

LUCA

IT'S LATE. My watch tells me it's after one a.m., so I haven't slept in over twenty-four hours. Things needed to be taken care of before I got that option. I shut the door to the bedroom behind me and lock it. I'm removing my gun from my holster when the bedside lamp turns on.

Haven sits up. With her eyes wide open and lips set in a

hard line, it's clear she's been waiting for me. "Why didn't you tell me about Nite?"

I place my gun on the nightstand. I see my sister and her have been chatty. "Didn't seem important."

She gasps. "They cut out his tongue, Luca. They—"

"I know what they did, Haven," I interrupt her. I'm not in the mood to do this with her. She slept on the plane, but I didn't, so I'm pissy and tired. Not a good combination.

"Mia told me that you, Nite, and another guy took care of the ones who hurt him."

I nod.

"What did you do to them?" she asks.

"You don't want to know."

"I do."

"No, you don't," I growl, removing my shirt.

She runs a hand through her dark hair. "I don't understand. How did you know to come here?"

"Yesterday when I was meeting with Bones, he informed me that there had been talk. Rossi had men together, and they were ready. He suggested they might come after you, but I know who they would go after."

"Mia," she whispers.

I nod.

"Why don't we stay here with her?"

"It's not safe. I have to go back. *We* have to go back. I have businesses to run, and we have a wedding to celebrate. If I stay too long, they'll start asking questions and possibly track me, which would lead them right to her."

"Bring her back to Vegas with us," she argues.

"I can't."

"Call your father. You had him send her here, so you can talk to him ..."

"I can't!" I shout. "I'm not her father. I have no control

over her." She doesn't know what it feels like to have your hands tied. I've spent all my life protecting Mia. From the moment I saw her, I knew I was all she had.

Six years old

"PLEASE ..." MY MOTHER CRIES. "I'M BEGGING YOU."

I knock on the door before twisting the knob and entering. Not waiting for permission. My mother lies in the center of the large bed. A woman stands off to the side, a crying baby cradled in her arms.

My sister.

No one pays me any attention.

My father walks over to the woman who has been staying at our house for the last month to help my mother get ready for the baby. "Let me have her." He holds out his hands.

The woman hands her over, and my mom shifts on the bed. "Please!" she cries. "Don't do this! Not again ..."

"Silence!" he barks, causing her to push herself into the headboard. He holds my sister in his arms, softly rocking her back and forth. A smile spreads across his face as he stares down at my little sister, and it makes me nervous. I've seen that look before. It's the same one he gives before he takes a life. "She may stay," he finally says, and my mother begins to sob. "But a time will come when she will earn her last name."

"Yes." My mother nods, brushing the tears from her cheeks. "Of course."

"SHE CAN LIVE WITH US. I'LL HELP HIDE HER," HAVEN goes on, cutting through my thoughts.

"No," I growl.

"Luca ..."

"Do you know what I had to do in order to get him to put her here?" I snap.

"What? Luca?" She gets up on her knees. "What did you do?"

I shake my head. I can't tell her. I can't let her know. She'll never forgive me. My sister will never forgive me. "It doesn't matter. It's done."

She slams her fists in my chest. "That's the same thing my father said to me before he gave me over to you," she yells.

"Listen."

"She can't live here. She's isolated."

I'm getting a headache. "She's safe."

"That's no life."

"Tell that to the thousands of Mafia women who have been beaten and raped." Her eyes widen. "Tell that to the ones who were sold into sex slavery. Or the ones thrown in a jail cell for crimes they never committed." I sigh, rubbing my temples. "Tomorrow morning, we are getting on that plane, and we will leave Mia here."

Tears fill her eyes. "Just when I was starting to tolerate you, you remind me of who you are. And I remember just how much I hate you." She jumps out of bed, rushes out of the room, and slams the door behind her. I have no desire to fight with her or even try to explain the Bianchi way of life to her, so I let her go.

ELEVEN

HAVEN

I STORM THROUGH the large house and toward the kitchen. Flipping on the light, I shriek when I run into a small body.

"I'm so sorry," Mia rushes out. "I didn't mean to frighten you."

"You're fine," I tell her, letting out a long breath. "What are you doing up so late?" I ask, noticing that she's changed out of her bathing suit into a purple silk nightgown. It has lace straps; one has fallen off her shoulder. The hem touches the floor, but it has a long slit up her side, showing off her thigh. Her face is clear of any makeup, yet she still looks runway ready.

"Can't sleep. You?"

"Same," I mumble. I think all that sleep I got on the plane screwed me over. Then add in the time change and all the new information I've learned. Any one of those things could be the cause.

"Want me to make you something?" she offers.

"Oh, no. You don't have to do that."

"Nonsense." She waves me off. "Do you like biscuits and gravy?"

I smile. "They're my favorite."

"Then that's what I'll make."

"Do you cook a lot?" I ask, pulling out a barstool and sitting down at the kitchen island.

She nods, grabbing stuff from the stainless fridge. "I love it. I have a lot of time on my hands, so over the years, I've learned to cook all sorts of food."

"Do you go to college?" I ask, being nosy.

She snorts. "I wish. I'm not allowed to go to school."

"What do you mean not allowed?" I don't know much about Italian education.

"Women in my family aren't supposed to have a brain." She rolls her eyes. "I never even went to high school." My eyes widen. "I had nannies who taught me all that I know, which I'm afraid isn't much." She smiles at me. "I'd love to go to college. Not only to learn, but the parties." Placing her elbows on the island, she drops her chin into her hands, giving me a smile that lights up her face. It makes her look younger than I know she is. "Do you have any wild stories you can tell me?"

I laugh, thinking about the time me and Emilee were with Bones and Luca in the game room. "Not that you'd want to hear."

She frowns.

"They involve your brother," I inform her.

Her face scrunches. "Yeah, I don't care to hear those." And then she straightens herself.

"So you're here all alone?" I change the subject.

"No. There are always guards and house cleaners. The twins are somewhere around here tearing up Italy. They come and go."

I thought my father selling me was bad, but he didn't ship me off alone and forget about me. This girl has been completely abandoned. She's been left in her own world and closed off from anyone. "What about your mother?"

She shakes her head. "My father won't allow her to leave New York. She rarely gets to go to Vegas."

Fucker!

"Boys?"

A blush fills her cheeks. "Oh, no."

This woman is so innocent. "Have you ever been on a date?"

She shakes her head and laughs. "No."

"Oh, you like someone, though," I observe. I know the look a girl has when she's got a crush. "Who is it?" I know it's no one I would know, but again, this is just me being nosy. And plus, it's felt like forever since I've had some girl talk. "Tell me all about him."

"Well ..." She bites her bottom lip. "I've never told anyone this, but I've always liked Oliver."

My eyes widen. "You have a crush on Nite?"

"Shh." She laughs softly, her eyes darting around the large kitchen, but we're all alone. "He would never like me, though."

What? "Mia. You're absolutely gorgeous. Not that looks have everything to do with it, but he'd be lucky to be with you."

She averts her eyes to the kitchen island. "You're lucky, you know? With Luca. That he got to pick you."

"What do you mean?"

"In our world, our father chooses who their children will marry and what families will be connected. Luca has loved you for a long time, and while he was here, he spent the entire time looking for a way to make you his wife."

"Here?" My eyes widen, and I release a long breath. "That's why he came to Italy? It was to be with you." I answer my own question.

She gives me a sad smile. "He was a total grouch the whole time. I called him sour tart."

I laugh, trying to imagine Luca allowing anyone to call him that. "Sour tart?"

She nods. "You know those sour candies that makes your face twist? He walked around like that all the time. He hated leaving you. He hated lying to you even more."

My chest tightens.

"He was on a mission."

"To what?"

"To find out what leverage he needed to get you." My heart beats faster. "Father had a woman chosen for him, but Luca wasn't having it." Her lips pull back. "Thank God. Maria wasn't right for him."

I totally ignore the fact that she just said their father wanted him to marry someone else because that doesn't matter. Obviously, Luca got what he wanted—me. "Do you know what he found?"

She shakes her head. "No. But I knew the moment he found what he was looking for because he no longer wore that sour look. He wasn't smiling and bouncing around the house or anything, but he was determined. He packed up his stuff and left weeks later."

I sit back in my seat, my chest heavy.

"Hey, I'm sorry I upset you."

"No." I shake my head. "I'm sorry I took him from you."

She gives me a soft smile. "Luca was always supposed to be where you were."

LUCA

I FEEL THE bed dip, and then the covers are yanked away. "Haven ..." My voice trails off as she straddles my hips. "What are you doing?" I ask roughly, starting to fully wake from my sleep. The room is pitch black, so I know it's not morning yet. After she stormed out of the room, I didn't bother to go after her. I got into bed and passed the fuck out.

Her small hands make their way up my sides and over my chest. Then she drags her nails down over my skin. I hiss in a breath at the sharpness.

"Haven ... what are you—"

"Shh," she interrupts me. Then I feel her chest on top of mine.

I lift my hands, and they tangle in her hair before her lips softly touch mine. "Don't ruin this," she whispers.

"Ruin what?" I ask, wondering where this is going.

"You. Me. Us," she answers, trailing her lips down my jawline and to my neck. She kisses my skin, and I push her head downward with my hands still in her hair. My cock is hard. Has been since I felt her on top of me.

She gets the hint and moves lower. Her hand grips the base of my cock, and I feel her tongue circle my head, but I change my mind.

I push her off me and onto her back. She doesn't protest. She knows I'm not in the mood for foreplay.

Grabbing her thighs, I shove them to her chest and stomach. I take my cock in my hand and rub it against her pussy. She's wet, just as I knew she would be. I push into her, and she whimpers. I reach around and grab her arms, pulling them across her legs and pin them down parallel.

I can hear her panting. The room fills with soft noises of her struggle at this angle. I have her caged in. Tilting her ass a little bit, I start to fuck her.

TWELVE

HAVEN

I LIE NEXT to him, my heart still pounding, and my body covered in sweat. I turn onto my side and watch him. He has his eyes shut, lips parted, and hand on his chest. My eyes have adjusted to the darkness, allowing me to see better.

"What did you do?" I find myself unable to hold it in any longer. I need to know.

He opens his eyes, then turns his head to look at me. "You're gonna have to be more specific."

I sit up and push my wild hair from my sweaty face. "What did you do in order to get my father to agree to force me to marry you?"

He closes his eyes and sighs. "Haven—"

"I won't be mad at you," I interrupt him, trying to assure him that he can tell me. "Please?" He looks back up at me, and I straddle his hips, shoving my hair behind my ear. "I want to know. I think I deserve that." I go another route. Anything to get him to open up to me.

He places his hands on my hips and releases a sigh. His

dark eyes roam my face before they meet mine. "I black-mailed him."

I keep my face blank of emotion. He's being very vague. "Who gave you the information that you needed in order to do that?"

"Your mother."

My mouth falls open. "What?"

He gently runs his hands up and down my bare thighs. "Your mother called and informed me that your father was in debt. That he had been skimming from the bank for years. She wanted to protect you. Said that you weren't the same since I left, and that she knew a way I could get you back."

"She set me up?" I whisper.

He sits up, and I go to pull away, but he wraps his arm around my waist to hold me in place. "She knew I wouldn't walk away from you, and she knew you needed me."

"But you did walk away from me. And I was doing just fine without you," I add with bite. He frowns at me. "It all makes sense. Why my stuff was packed ... why she never tried to reach out to me ..." My voice trails off as my jaw tightens.

"Haven, she did this ..."

"For her!" I growl. "She didn't want Dad to lose her precious house. Her cars. Money. She wanted to make sure she had a backup plan."

"Haven ..."

"How do you know she wasn't screwing the banks too?"

"Haven ...?"

"Does my dad know?" I demand. "That she snitched on him?"

He shakes his head. "He knows that I know he's in debt and he needed an escape plan, but he has no idea who gave

156

me the intel. I'm not even sure he knows she's aware of what is going on with the banks."

"So ... what? You gave him five million, and all is good now?" I cross my arms over my chest.

His jaw sharpens, and he looks away from me.

"Luca ..."

"I gave him the money in exchange for you and control over all fifteen locations."

I nod my head once. "To launder money through." It's what the Mafia does. So much of their income comes from drugs and other illegal activities. Cash. They have to hide it from the government, and my father's misfortune was Luca's ticket.

"What do you expect?" He growls. "For me to live on the straight and narrow?" He cups my face with his free hand. "I love you, Haven. Always have. Always will. I won't sit here and apologize for finding a way to get you. And if that means I get to make a little money in the meantime, then so be it."

I bite my bottom lip. "Why five million?"

He gives me a smile. The one I never could tell no. "Because that's how deep he was." He grabs my left hand and looks at my ring. "But I would have paid a billion if it meant you were going to be mine forever."

I fall down onto the bed next to him, and he pulls me into his side. "What about Mia?" I ask. She's at risk. I'm just not sure from what yet.

He stiffens. "What about her?"

"Why does your father hide her here?"

He lets out a long sigh. "A player never shows his hand."

The same thing Mia had told me. I close my eyes, hating those words because I know exactly what they mean. "He's going to use her. Just like my father used me." Women are handed over like poker chips. She'll be married off to a man to benefit his father. They're always trying to climb the ranks. Doesn't matter how much money they have or how big their mansions are, they always want more. And they use others to profit from it.

He doesn't say anything, but what is there to say? It wasn't a question. And I vow to myself that whatever ends up happening to her, I'll be there. I may not be able to stop it, but I will not let her feel helpless or lost. I'll make sure she knows she will always have someone she can call. Who she can run to. I'll protect her when no one else will. I'll be the best damn sister since Lord knows her brothers are shit.

I push off the bed, trying to sit up, but he wraps his arms around my waist and pulls me down. His hand runs up and down my stomach, and a thought hits me. "Why don't we use a condom?" We never were careful, but the fact that the paperwork mentioned heirs makes me think he wants me to get pregnant now. I don't remember it saying when I had to produce children. I would think a shotgun wedding would look bad for him and the Bianchi family. But even if I was already knocked up, the wedding is in less than two weeks, so I wouldn't be showing that fast. And they could always lie and say I had the baby earlier than my delivery date. Happens all the time.

"Because I know you're on the shot." He yawns.

"What? How?" Not the answer I was expecting.

"I know that you see Dr. Nelson every three months. Have been since ... well, you know."

I'm not sure what to say to that. I lay my head on his chest and listen to his breathing even out until he slightly snores. And I let out a long sigh. He's right. I've been on the shot for four years now.

. . .

"Haven, what's wrong?" Emilee asks, her heels clanking on the floor while she tries to keep up with me.

"I need the bathroom," I answer, hurrying.

"Are you gonna get sick?"

We round the corner and come to a quick stop when we see one of the Kings leaning up against the men's bathroom door, holding it closed.

Titan has his arms crossed over his chest, left foot planted on the floor while his right knee is bent, and his black boot is resting on the door behind him. And he has a sucker in his mouth. The moment he sees us, he reaches up and pulls it out with a pop. "What are you two doing out of class?" he questions.

I don't answer and neither does Emilee because she doesn't know why I dragged her down the hallway. I picked the least busy hall this early in the morning. College students still roam the halls, but it's dead right now.

His eyes move from mine to hers. He looks her up and down, lingering on her chest and thighs for a few extra seconds. When they reach her lips, he licks his.

I look at her with raised brows. What have I missed? She turns her head but not before I see the blush on her face.

A noise from inside the bathroom has me taking a step toward him. "What's going on in there?"

"Nothing. Move along." Then he winks at Emilee. "You can stay. Need a reminder ...?"

"Titan ..." She growls but there's a blush again.

What the hell?

The door opens a tad, but Titan holds it shut with his weight. And I finally understand. The Kings must be in there, beating the shit out of some unlucky soul. It happens. Often. The Dark Kings are bullies. They will make you

159

bleed. No matter if it's with their fists or a knife. I once heard that Cross burned a guy on the face with a cigarette.

Without caring what's going on, I reach over and grab E's hand, yanking her into the women's bathroom. I rush into a stall. "What was that about?" I ask, undoing my jeans.

She sighs. "Well, you know last weekend when we fucked the guys in the game room at the party?"

"Yeah," I answer slowly, wondering where she's going with that.

"That wasn't the first time I've had an audience."

I nod to myself. "I remember you and Bones mentioning that." I unzip my backpack and pull out a tampon before I finish up in the stall.

"Yeah, well ..." She pauses when I exit. "Before that, I let Bones fuck me in the men's locker room after school hours."

I remember that too. It was when I was mad at Luca and thought he was texting me, but it was her phone going off. "That's nothing new." I snort washing my hands.

"Yeah, but Titan was in there and watched us."

"What?"

She bites her bottom lip. "At the time, I didn't think Bones knew, but what he said in the game room last weekend confirmed that he knew Titan was in there watching us."

I stare at her wide-eyed. "Well ... Are you mad at Bones?"

"No. Should I be?"

I chuckle, yanking towels out of the dispenser.

"I ... uh, I ..."

"What?" I turn to face her. "Spit it out." She knows she can tell me anything. The girls and I don't keep secrets from one another.

"I wanted him to join us," she admits.

My eyes bug out. I was not expecting that to come out of her mouth.

"I know." She places her hands over her face. "I'm such a slut."

"Hey." I pull them away. "You are not a slut. You've only ever slept with Bones. It's totally understandable to want to try out another dick."

She laughs.

"There's nothing wrong with being sexually hungry, E."

She looks down at the floor and nods once.

"And Bones obviously seems okay with it. Maybe you should offer—"

"Absolutely not!" she interrupts me, turning to face the mirror. She slides her hand down her white Gucci dress. "Enough about me. Let's talk about you."

"I've never had a three-way," I admit. And although I was one hundred percent turned on when I watched Bones fuck her, I have no interest in a threesome.

She rolls her eyes. "No, I mean why did we have to skip class to rush in here? Did you pee your pants?" She chuckles softly. "Or were you afraid you were going to shit yourself?"

"Oh. I had started my period."

She frowns. "I'm not on."

We've been on the same cycle for almost a year now. Poor Jasmine has never had one the same time each month. "I know. I've been sweating bullets, thinking I was pregnant."

"What?" She gasps.

"It was a false alarm." I shrug like it's no big deal, but I've been nervous as fuck. We don't always use condoms, and I also don't take my pills religiously. Plus, I was drinking at the party. I didn't realize I was late until a few days after.

"Why didn't you tell me? And what would you have

done?" she asks wide-eyed.

I shrug. "I hadn't thought that far."

Throwing her head back, she sighs. "See, this is why I can't afford a threesome. What if I got pregnant and didn't know who the dad was? Bones and I don't use condoms. Well, we did in the beginning but not anymore."

I don't say anything. It sounds so irresponsible when she puts it that way.

"Come on, let's go to class," she orders.

We walk out of the women's bathroom, but my upper arm is grabbed, and I'm pulled to a stop.

"Haven." Luca stands there in the busy hall, his dark eyes boring down on mine. "May I speak to you?"

"I'm late ..."

"It'll only take a minute." He yanks me back into the bathroom, then locks the door behind us, shutting Emilee out.

"I'll see you in class," she calls out through the door.

"I'm on my period," I tell him. "We can't have bathroom sex."

"I know. We heard you girls."

"You heard ...?" My voice trails off when I realize what he means. Narrowing my eyes, I demand. "Were you in the men's bathroom with the Kings?"

The rooms share a wall. I didn't hear them, but I wasn't really listening either. Now I know it's because after they were beating the shit out of some guy, they were spying on us.

He doesn't answer. But he doesn't have to. I already know that answer. "You had no right ..."

"You should have told me you thought you were pregnant," he snaps.

"Why? To push you away?"

He lets out a long sigh and steps into me. Cupping my cheeks, he frowns. "You think I'd leave you?"

"*The thought crossed my mind,*" I admit softly. *I've taken five pregnancy tests, and they all said negative, but none of them helped ease my fear. What my mom would say. How I would tell him. It has consumed my every thought. I think to the point that I was convincing my body I was growing a baby. The stress alone probably kept me from starting.*

"*Haven, I'm never going to leave you.*" *He pulls me into him.* "*I just wish you would have told me. My job is to take care of you. And if we get pregnant, then I'll take care of both of you.*"

"*If we get pregnant?*" *I arch a brow.*

"*Of course. You're not alone in this relationship, Haven.*"

I WENT THAT VERY NEXT DAY TO GET ON THE SHOT. I told my mother about my pregnancy scare and that I had missed some pills, so I chose the shot instead. I wonder how long I'll be able to keep getting them. "I didn't read the contract," I blurt out. I need him to understand that I don't know all that is required of me.

He stays silent, but he's no longer snoring, so I know I woke him up.

"I do love you," I whisper. "And I'd love to have a family with you, but I won't allow you to harm any child of mine."

He shifts, and I close my eyes.

"Haven. Haven, look at me," he orders, placing his hand on my face to tilt it toward him.

I open my eyes, and they sting from unshed tears. "I may be my father's son, but I'm nothing like him. I don't want my parents' marriage. And I would never, ever hurt you or our children." He presses his lips gently to my forehead, and the first tear rolls down the side of my face.

THIRTEEN

HAVEN

The following morning, we told Mia and Nite goodbye. She hugged me tight and asked me to take care of Luca. I promised her that I would do my best. An hour later, we boarded the same private jet we took here with my two new bodyguards and headed back to Nevada. I slept most of the time. I messaged Jasmine and tried to call Emilee, but her phone was still off. And I hated it. I just wanted to hear her voice. I needed her to know that I was there for her, even if she didn't want to be found.

After we arrived back in the States and made our way back to Luca's, I showered and passed out. The next day, I woke up with a new determination. We had less than two weeks before our wedding, and I was going to willingly walk down that aisle with a genuine smile on my face, but I needed to take care of something first. It was inevitable, so I might as well do it sooner rather than later.

I pull my black Mercedes up to the valet at the country club where I grew up. I step out and throw the guy my keys. Stomping up the stairs, I push my sunglasses to the top of my head.

Walking in, I look around at all the men and women who occupy the facility, and I wonder how many are like my father. Living a lie? How many would sell their only child to get out of debt? I bet my life every last son of a bitch here would.

I make my way through the place and down a hallway. I take the first right and open the door to the Cayman's spa. I know she's here. She's never missed a Monday appointment. Just as I walk up to the circular desk, she calls my name.

"Haven?"

I spin around to see my mother walking toward me with a smile on her face and her arms out wide. She looks like she just returned from a beach vacation. Her crimson dress hugs her hips and chest, showing off her assets. She wears black Gucci sandals and a Louis Vuitton on her shoulder.

I place my hands on my hips. "So you sold me out in order to keep your skin looking young?"

Her face instantly falls.

Luca was right when we stood in his bathroom the night of our engagement party. *He's all that I have.*

The one person in the world who was supposed to love me dropped me off at a fire station. Growing up, my mom and dad were very open about how they adopted me. They told me that if I ever wanted to find my birth mother, they would help me. I didn't. If she didn't want me then, she wouldn't want me now. So we swept it all under the rug.

They always told me that I was a miracle from God. They had been trying for children for years and couldn't have a baby. The woman standing in front of me, who I grew up calling mom, had three miscarriages. Then one day, my father got a phone call from his friend that he had taken an abandoned baby to the hospital. My parents showed up three hours later with an attorney. When you have money, the red tape isn't as thick. They took me home the following day and raised me as their own. They gave me their last name and a beautiful life.

Under the Safe Haven law, you are able to drop off a baby in a safe manner without fear of prosecution up to thirty days after birth. Hence why my parents named me Haven.

I grew up hearing I love you every second of every day. My parents showered me with kisses and hugs. But look where that got me.

"Haven ..."

"Why did you do it?" I ask. My voice is trembling, and I hate that it makes me look like I care. I clear my throat. "Was it for your membership here at the club? The expensive cars? The mansions and yachts?" I rattle off anything I can think of them losing.

"No." She gasps.

"Was it because Daddy told you to?" I continue trying to think of every scenario. He looked too happy about the situation when I stood in his office and he forced my name to the paperwork. He didn't act like Luca was buying me. More like he offered me. Maybe he and my mother had a plan that Luca didn't know about.

She drops her eyes to the floor, and I raise a brow. "He doesn't know."

Luca didn't tell me much information about it, but then again, I wasn't exactly sure how much I wanted to know.

"You love Luca," she finally says.

"And that makes this okay?" I ask, throwing my arms out to my side.

When she takes a step toward me, I take one back, matching it. "He can give you a life that we never could."

"What are you talking about?" I ask confused. "You gave me a great life." They weren't overly affectionate with one another, but I never saw them fight or even argue. I was a spoiled rich kid who didn't want for anything. Even after high school, I went on to college. I dropped out my senior year after Luca left me, but they never made me get a job. Nothing. I didn't grow up in the real world. Mine has always been full of plastic cards that didn't have limits. I had the best friends a girl could ask for. What could he possibly offer me that they can't?

Her eyes dart around the lobby of the spa before she grabs my upper arm and yanks me into a nearby room. It has a rock wall that water cascades down into a small pool, and a black leather massage chair sits next to it. The sound would be soothing if I wasn't so pissed.

"Listen, Haven." She licks her lips, her eyes pleading with me. "I did what needed to be done. And one day when you become a mother, you will understand."

"Mom ..."

"You needed to be a Bianchi."

My confusion deepens along with my brows. "You're not making any sense."

She pulls me in for a hug, holding me tightly. My arms stay down to my side, feeling heavy. "I love you, Haven. Just remember that. No matter what, I love you." She pulls back and looks me in the eye. Hers are filled with tears. "You were always meant to be my daughter. And I know that no matter what happens, Luca will take care of you." She reaches up and pushes some stray hairs behind my ear. "He will make a great husband and a loving father." She gives me a sad smile. "He can give you things that I never could."

"Mom ..."

The door to the room bursts open, and my two new bodyguards enter.

"We found her, sir," Max says into his cell phone.

"Did you follow me?" I demand.

My mom pulls away from me and turns to face them just as the guy hangs up his phone. "You need to come with us, Haven," he orders.

I take a step back. "I'm not going anywhere with you," I snap. "I'm here to see my mother. Tell Luca that I'll be home once I'm done."

He shakes his head. "I'm afraid I can't do that. We were given orders ..."

"And I'm telling you that I will be home when I'm done," I snap.

"Haven ..." My mother grabs my hands and tightens her hold on them. "Go home."

"But Mom ..."

She pulls me in for another hug, squeezing me so tight that she takes my breath away. I hear her sniff in my ear. "Let him protect you, baby. Let him do his job."

I barge into the house and head straight to his office with my two babysitters right on my ass. I know that's where he is. I shove open the door to find him alone, sitting behind his desk on his phone. He doesn't even bother looking up at me. I walk up to it and slam my palms down on the surface.

"I'll have to call you back," he says into his cell.

"What the hell do you think you're doing?" I demand the moment he sets it down.

His eyes go to the two idiots who I know are standing

behind me. He gives them a nod, and then I hear the door shut when they let themselves out.

"Funny." He leans back in his seat, glaring up at me. "I can ask you the same question."

"I was talking to my mother," I snap. "Not running away."

"You went without protection."

I snort and shove off his desk. "I don't need them breathing down my neck."

"Haven—" He stands.

"No," I interrupt him. "I'm serious, Luca. I will not let you treat me like your father treats Mia." His eyes narrow on me. "I won't allow you to ..."

"To what?" he growls. "Keep you safe?"

"Make me a prisoner," I correct him.

He runs a hand over his face and lets out a sigh. "Haven, there are things going on that you don't know about."

"You mean the six men you slaughtered years ago and now their leader is after you for revenge?" I arch a brow. "Or how about when you left me and made me think it was for another woman?" I yell. "You could have just told me about Mia. I would have kept your secret or went with you, but you didn't even stop to think of that as an option."

"You were in college."

"I dropped out anyway!"

He nods once, and his jaw clenches. "Is this how our marriage is going to go? Always bringing up the past?"

I say nothing.

"Oh? So it's like that?"

"Yes." I cross my arms over my chest. "It's like that."

He walks around his desk and pushes his body into

mine. I glare up at him. "You don't want to challenge me, Haven."

"What are you going to do to me, Luca? Send me to my room? Take away my phone? Make my two babysitters watch my every move?"

He lifts his hand and instinct has me flinching.

His hand pauses by my face, and I realize that he was just going to tuck some hair behind my ear, but the damage is done. I thought he was going to hit me, and he knows it.

He fists his hand, snatching it back, and places both hands in the front pockets of his slacks.

We stand in an uncomfortable silence for a few seconds before he turns, giving me his back, and sits at his desk. "You are no longer allowed to leave the house."

"Luca—"

"You will not leave this house!" he shouts, interrupting me. "Not without the guys at your side. And you will stay the hell away from your mother."

"Excuse me?"

"I mean it, Haven. It's an order."

He did not just say that. "An order. You will not ..."

"Since when do you want to see her anyway?" He arches a brow. "You hated her just last week. All of a sudden, she's your best fucking friend."

"She's my mother!"

He snorts. "Since when does that mean anything?"

I throw my arms up, not in the mood to have this conversation with him. Without another word, I turn around and storm out of his office.

LUCA

I LEFT HAVEN back at the house to stew. All of a

sudden, she wants to be best friends with her mother, and I don't like it. I park my car behind Kingdom and run up the stairs. I had been on the phone with Bones when Haven entered my office at home. He said he needed to see me, so here I am.

"Hello, sir," Nigel greets me.

"Is Bones upstairs?"

"He's in the meat locker, sir."

Hmm. *Wonder who the unlucky bastard is?*

"I will escort you." He walks out from behind the desk and over to the single elevator. Using his key card, he presses the lowest level, and it begins to descend. "You have a good evening, sir," he says as the door slides open.

I nod to him. "You too, Nigel." Exiting the elevator, I walk down the long hallway. Coming to the end, I twist the knob and push the door open. Stepping into the cold room, I allow the heavy metal door to close behind me. I see Bones standing in the middle of the room with his hands in the pockets of his dress slacks, staring down at a man who is on his knees. A man I know well.

Marco.

"You're out of time," Bones tells him. "And I had to track you down. Know what that means?"

Marco just shakes his head.

"Means I get to break your hands."

"No. No. You said if I didn't sign the paper, you would break my hands, but I signed it." His eyes go from Bones to mine. They plead with me as if he thinks I came to save him.

I didn't.

"I guess that makes you a thief and me a liar," Bones states.

"Wait. Wait. I can get your money."

"Obviously, you couldn't, or you would have."

"What can I do?" he begs wide-eyed.

"There's nothing you can do now. You're out of time." Bones steps up to him, grabs his right hand, and bends it back. The sound of bones breaking bounces off the concrete walls.

Marco screams out in agony, throwing his head back. "It was only five grand," he cries, now cradling his broken wrist.

Bones places his hands back in the pockets of his slacks. "I would have broken it for five dollars," he states. "It's the principle. Now I'll give you three days to pay it, or I'll break the other one. Understand?"

FOURTEEN

HAVEN

I PACE BACK and forth in our room, mad at Luca. Who is he to tell me what I should and shouldn't feel? Yes, she is the reason I'm here, and although I was mad at her, I don't hate her. Not now. Not after I found out about his sister. What he has done for her and how she described how he missed me. I thought he had left me and never looked back, but obviously, that was not the case.

My cell begins to ring, and I look down at it to see it's a blocked number. Biting my bottom lip, I debate after a few seconds but press answer. Maybe it's Mia.

"Hello?"

"Haven."

I frown at the male's voice knowing my name. He doesn't sound familiar. "Who is this?" I ask, doing a three-sixty of our bedroom to make sure I'm alone.

"Someone who has all the answers," he says cryptically.

I sit down on the end of the bed. "All the answers regarding what?"

"Meet me tomorrow."

"I don't think so." I go to hang up, but his next words stop me.

"I can tell you everything you need to know about your soon-to-be husband."

"Tell me what exactly?" I ask, my heart pounding.

Is he having an affair with a married woman? There's so much I don't know about him. And I never expected him to be celibate while we were apart, so who knows what all he did?

"Tomorrow. In person. There will be a car waiting for you at 4th and Lexington."

"A car?" I ask. That's just a couple of blocks from Luca's house. "I can't. The house is full of …"

"I'll take care of it."

My brows pull together. *Who the fuck is this guy?* "Take care of what?"

"A distraction. I know he's got you on 24-hour surveillance. He'll be at Glass. I'll give you a five-minute window."

"Wait?" I jump to my feet. "Glass? The strip club? Why would he be there?" Who the hell would he be up there meeting that early?

There's a short pause on his end. "He keeps everything from you, doesn't he?" His voice has an edge to it. As if he's mad at Luca. "He owns the club. Why else would he be there at eight a.m.?"

I shake my head to myself. "No. I think you're mistaking …"

"I'm not. Now, eight a.m. tomorrow. Don't be late." Then he hangs up.

Staring down at my phone, I see the screen and wonder what the hell just happened. Who the hell was that? And why the hell does Luca own a strip club that he hasn't told me about?

I DIDN'T SLEEP A WINK LAST NIGHT. I HAD CRAWLED into bed after I received the phone call and pretended to be asleep when Luca finally arrived home. He showered, then came to bed. He kissed my shoulder good night, and it wasn't long after that before he started to snore. Then again, this morning, he woke up, got ready, and kissed me goodbye. The entire time, I faked being asleep. And true to the random stranger's word, the house was silent. Not a soul to be found. I checked all over. I walked right out the front door and down the driveway before walking through the open gate. It was somewhat scary. Had the guy placed a bomb threat? Wouldn't they have escorted me off the grounds if that were the case? I kept waiting on my cell to ring, for Luca to call me and ask if I was okay. If they had an emergency on the property, wouldn't he want to make sure I was safe?

True to the guy's word, a car was waiting for me. I got in the back seat, and a male sat in the driver's seat. He didn't say anything to me. Just put the car in gear and drove off.

I quickly look around as he pulls into the back of a parking lot. It looks to be a two-story red brick building with a white door. The car comes to a stop, and the guy just sits behind the wheel. The door unlocks, and I take that as my cue to get the hell out.

I open the car door just as the back door to the building opens. A guy dressed in a three-piece black suit stands there, holding it ajar for me. He looks like a million bucks. No street thug wears Armani suits and a Rolex watch.

"Did you call me?" I ask him.

He doesn't answer. His black shades hide his eyes from me, but he jerks his head toward the building.

I take a deep breath and step inside. He grips my upper arm and pulls me farther into a hallway.

"Hey," I snap, trying to pull free, but he just tightens his hold. "Let me go!" I shout.

"Do as she says," a man orders as we enter a room.

I come to a quick stop, and a gasp escapes my lips before I can stop it when I see the man who spoke. He sits behind a desk, his arms crossed over his chest while he leans causally back in his black leather chair. His dark eyes stare into mine, challenging me.

Oh, fuck!

I have made a grave mistake. I spin around to leave, but the muscle steps between me and the door, keeping me hostage. "Let me out!" I shout.

"So you know me?" the guy sitting behind the desk asks casually. His heart obviously not pounding like mine.

I spin back around to face him. All I can do is nod. Luca would kill me if he knew I was here. If this guy doesn't do it for him. "Why am I here?" I swallow hard.

"I think we can help each other," he says, eyeing me up and down.

"I won't help you," I growl.

There's only one thing this guy could want from me, and I refuse to give him any intel on Luca. Or maybe he wants to know about Mia. We did just go see her, and she informed me of how Nite wouldn't give her up, and they took his tongue for it.

"What if I told you I know who your mother is? Your biological mother?"

His words make my heart stop. My mind races. "My

mother?" I ask, blinking. All of a sudden, I'm interested in what he has to say.

Your mother gave you up. Abandoned you. It doesn't matter who she is, she doesn't want to know me. Or me know her. I shake my head. "I know who my mother is." I've wondered why my biological mother gave me up, and the best I could come up with is that she knew my life was better off without her. Maybe she had an incurable disease and couldn't take care of me. Maybe she was an addict. Maybe she had been raped and couldn't stand to look at me—a reminder of what had happened to her. Or maybe, she just didn't want me. Either way, I came to live with her decision a long time ago. And I was at peace with it.

A slow and mischievous grin spreads across his face. Alberto Rossi doesn't look anything like Luca's father. He may be the leader of the second largest organized crime operation in Las Vegas, but he doesn't have the large belly and sweat-covered forehead. He keeps himself in shape. He has been feuding with the Bianchis for years, and somehow, he knows my real mother? This has to be a trick.

It's a lie, a trap to get me here, and I fell for it.

"That is correct. You do know your mother." He tilts his head to the side, and his dark eyes run up and down my body. It makes the hairs on the back of my neck stand up. "You look just like her."

I blink. My legs want to turn and run, but my mind is not letting me leave. It's as if I'm paralyzed where I stand. I've always wondered where she was and why she gave me up. If I looked like her, or if my voice sounded like hers. It was a thought that always sat in the back of my mind.

He stands from his chair and walks around his desk. My heart picks up as he nears me. But still, I can't seem to find the will to leave. Instead, I wait, frozen in my spot, needing him to speak. To tell me everything he knows.

Reaching out, he pushes some brown strands behind my right ear, and I take in a shaky breath. "She's lied to you all these years." He sighs. "I wanted to tell you. I thought you deserved to know. And now ..." He trails off as his jaw sets in a hard line. "It's time," he snaps, making me jump.

"For what?" I manage to get out.

"That you know everything." He gives me a soft smile. "And don't worry. We'll take them down. They won't even see us coming."

LUCA

I sit in the office of Glass behind my desk while Bones sits across from me. He's counting out the cash Marco delivered first thing this morning. It's funny how much money a man can find when broken bones are involved. The door to the office swings open, hitting the interior wall. Bones has already pulled out his gun from the holster on his hip as I reach for mine under the desk when we see Haven burst into the room.

"What are you doing here?" I demand, jumping from my chair. I haven't told her anything about this club, so how did she find me? Did she follow me this morning? Has she been following me?

Her wide eyes go from mine to Bones. He stays seated in his chair, but his brows are raised. He still holds his gun, but now it rests on his thigh.

She swallows nervously as the door shuts behind her. Her once olive skin tone is now white. It looks like she's seen a ghost. I take a step toward her, rounding the desk. "Haven ..."

"I didn't know what to say." She stumbles backward. Her back hitting the closed door. "I ... He ..."

"What?" I ask. "Who is he?"

She places her hand on her chest, and tears build in her brown eyes. "He wants you dead."

I stiffen.

Her eyes move to Bones. "All of you."

That brings him to his feet. "Who the fuck are you talking about?"

"Alberto Rossi."

I fist my hands, and Bones's brows pull together. "Although this isn't news, I would like to know who told you this?" he demands.

"He did."

"What?" I snap, making her jump.

She bows her head and sniffs, wrapping her arms around herself. "He told me who my mother is."

I run a hand through my hair. *What the fuck is she talking about?*

"When did you see him?" Bones asks. He looks at me. "Was he at your house?"

I shake my head. *Is he serious?* "I haven't seen him in years." He rarely comes to Vegas. Just like my father, they run their operations from long distances. My father lives in New York and very rarely visits Vegas. Their crew does their dirty work.

"He called me last night from a blocked number. Told me he would cause a diversion this morning so I could talk to him. A car would be waiting. I didn't know..."

What in the fuck? "You didn't fucking go, did you?" I bark out.

She nods quickly. "I didn't know it was him until I

arrived at a wedding chapel." She hiccups. "He told me he knew my real mother ..." She trails off.

"And?" Bones coaxes her. "Who is she?"

Wedding chapel? *Motherfucker!* He knows I was there the other night. Getting her to go to him willingly? He's sending me a warning.

Fuck.

Fuck.

Fuck.

"My mother."

"What are you talking about?" I demand. I'm pissed at her and confused as fuck. How did he get her number? Why did he reach out to her at all? It must be because of me. And how stupid could she be to fall for it? I never wanted to make her a prisoner in our home, but maybe that is what it's going to come down to in order to keep her alive.

"My adopted mother is my biological mother."

"I don't understand ..."

"My mother had an affair. Got pregnant with me."

"So who is your father?" Bones asks because I can't speak. I'm afraid I'll yell at her. Even in her fragile state, I want to rip her apart.

She takes in a deep breath. "Alberto Rossi."

FIFTEEN

HAVEN

A SILENCE FALLS over the large room. Both men stare at me with murderous eyes and fisted hands. I feel I may get sick. *Again.* I managed to hold my stomach while I stood in Rossi's ... my father's office at the wedding chapel/funeral home, but the moment I left and took a breath of fresh air, I lost everything I had eaten yesterday in the parking lot.

"He's lying." Bones shakes his head.

"He said there was a DNA test. That my mother has it." I didn't want to believe him, but the way he spoke about me. About my mother. As much as I wanted to deny it, I couldn't.

"That doesn't mean shit," Bones argues.

"Why in the fuck would you go and see him without telling me?" Luca finally finds his voice, yelling at me. "Do you have any idea what he could have done to you?"

"He doesn't want to hurt me."

"Bullshit!" he shouts.

I flinch but shake my head. "He wants to hurt you. He thinks I can help with that."

"How so?" Bones inquires.

"He thinks you're forcing me to marry you."

Like a rubber band, something snaps in Luca, and he comes for me. But Bones jumps between us and places his hands up to stop him. "It's believable. Have you seen the pictures circulating in the media of your engagement party? Haven looks every bit pissed off at you. As if she even loathes you. He could be buying it because it did come out of nowhere. For two years, the media has been talking about your absence, then you show up, and poof, you're engaged."

I don't state the obvious—that I did hate him at that point. That this is a contract. Luca may love me, but I'm still just a pawn in a game.

"What else did he say?" Bones goes on, keeping his back to me. He's so tall that I can't even see over him. So I stare at the bloody skull that covers up the entire back of his *Kingdom* T-shirt.

"He made a deal with my father. And he informed me that all I had to do was show up at the wedding, and he would take care of everyone there. It was going to be like shooting fish in a barrel. And I wouldn't be married off to a Bianchi."

I can't let him kill Luca. I love him. But the Kings? They have nothing to do with this feud the Bianchi family has with the Rossi family. Not that I know of. Yes, they're hated by most because of how powerful they are in this city, but that doesn't mean they should die. I grew up with them. I don't want their dead bodies on my conscience.

"And what did you tell him?" Bones goes on.

"What do you mean?" My voice shakes.

He turns around, and his blue eyes glare down at me. "I mean *what did you tell him*?"

"I told him what he wanted to hear," I admit, and my

shoulders fall. "That I would do as he said. I thought if I lied, I could buy you all time. A plan."

He nods and then steps away from me. My eyes now staring at Luca standing before me.

"Anything else he said that we can use?" Bones asks.

I look at him instead of Luca. "Yeah, he said he has eyes and ears everywhere. Even at Kingdom."

Bones doesn't waste a second; he pulls out his cell, dials up a number, and puts it to his ear. "Flush the system." Then he hangs up after giving whoever it was an order. Without another word, he exits, shutting me and Luca in the large room that seems to shrink by the second.

"I'm sorry," I say, hating the silence.

I take a step toward him, but when he steps back, tears fill my eyes. "I can't help who I am," I croak out.

His brows pull together. "You think I'm mad at you because he's filled your head with lies?" He shakes his head. "I'm pissed at you because you went behind my back. To a man who hates me and my family. My fucking name alone could get you killed! I'm a dead man to most in this city." He runs his hand through his hair aggressively. "Fuck! I thought you were smarter than this."

"I needed to know," I cry.

"Know what?" he screams. "About your biological mother? Since when do you fucking care about that?"

"About you!" I shout back, fisting my hands. "He started our conversation about you. How you owned Glass. How you were keeping secrets from me. He promised me answers. They just weren't what I wanted."

Giving me his back, he lets out a long breath, trying to calm his anger. He begins to pace back and forth. "He said he and your father have a deal?"

I don't miss how he avoids talking about him and this club. "Yes."

Pulling out his cell, he types out a quick message and then places it back in his pocket. "Did he say he would see you again?" he asks through clenched teeth.

"Not until the wedding."

He nods once. "Is he planning on keeping in contact?"

I shake my head. "He didn't say."

He comes over to me and takes my upper arm, ushering me out of the room and locking the office door behind us.

LUCA

SHE STAYS SILENT while I drive her back to our house. As soon as the car comes to a stop, I pull out my cell and send a text.

> Me: Get your ass home. Now!

Nite reads it immediately and responds.

> Nite: Yes, sir.

"Go straight to our room and do not leave," I tell her when we enter the house.

She stops and turns to face me. "Luca—"

"For the love of God, Haven, do as you're told. Just this once!" I shout.

She lifts her chin, crosses her arms over her chest, and storms up the stairs to our bedroom. I go straight to my office and open my gun safe. Pulling out my silencer, I tighten it on the end of my barrel and sit down behind my desk just as my door opens. My two newest bodyguards enter, both laughing like hyenas as they sit down across from me.

"Hey, Boss, what do you think about …?"

I shoot him in the head, then the other next to him. They both sit there dead. Their necks bent back at an odd angle from the force of my bullets at such a close range and blood dripping from their wounds onto my carpet. I'll have it ripped up tonight and replaced by tomorrow morning. Their arms hang down off the sides of the chairs.

They were rats.

They worked for Rossi. They had to be the ones. He told Haven he would create a diversion, and I never got a call that she was leaving the house. I never got a notification that my driver took her anywhere. They had set it all up. She never mentioned that she saw them, so they weren't personally involved. He just made sure to put them in the right position to give him what he wanted. Her. And they knew that she went to see her mother yesterday. I had them follow her and bring her back. Maybe they informed him they overheard her talking to her mother, and he got spooked, needed to make a play. Add that to the fact I raided his chapel, and it's all making sense.

I pull out my cell. It rings three times before the man answers. "Luca …"

"I flushed the system," I tell Titan.

"Take their phones. I'm sure they have to check in. We don't want to alert Rossi that they are no longer with us." He hangs up.

Two men he thought he trusted had been moles set in place months ago to give Rossi intel. He always hated that the Kings had loyalty to the Bianchi family. Who knows how long ago he set his plan in motion? Maybe he was using them to fuck over the Kings and just so happened to catch a break when Titan loaned them to me. Well, whatever plan he has, we're about to fuck it all up.

I BRING MY CAR TO A STOP OUTSIDE HER PARENTS' residence. Bones and I exit the car, and I grab the black bag from the back seat. I had messaged him before Haven and I ever left Glass and told him to be at my house at midnight tonight. I needed his help, and I knew he wouldn't let me down. He has just as much right to be here as I do. We're all on high alert.

We walk in like we own the place and climb the stairs. I know the bastard is here. And I also know he doesn't have much security. He never was smart. He and his wife are always carrying, but he's too cheap to hire men.

I open his office door without even knocking.

He looks up at me and Bones and smiles like the fucking fool he is. "Well, hello, boys. It's a little late for you all to be making house calls, isn't it?" He chuckles. "What can I do for you?"

"You could sign these for me." I toss a stack of papers onto the surface of his desk. I had my dear old friend Titan type me up some papers earlier while we figured out our plan.

He reaches for his glasses that sit on his desk and puts them on, squinting down at the papers. "What is this?"

"This ... is you signing over your shares to me."

"What?" He removes his glasses, confused, looking up at me.

I plop down in the seat across from him. "Bones."

He walks behind the desk to stand behind him. I throw him the duffel bag.

"I don't understand ..."

Bones pulls the plastic bag out of the duffel and places it over his head, yanking it back.

I lean over the desk and grip his wrists, pulling them across the surface to keep him from puncturing a hole in the bag. That would defeat the purpose. "Did you know that a brain can survive six minutes after the heart stops?"

Jimmy fights Bones, but he's not strong enough, not in this position. It would be a shitty way to die actually, given how easy it would be to survive. All you need to do is poke your finger through the plastic. It's not like it's Kevlar.

His head shakes back and forth, but it doesn't do him any good. His fight is useless. "Sign the papers," I order, letting go of his right hand to place a pen in his left. "And he'll let you go."

He aimlessly begins to write on his desk. I look up at Bones. "Let the man sign his name."

He removes the bag from his head, and Jimmy sucks in a deep breath, coughing.

"Sign it." I point at the yellow tab.

He scribbles his name down quickly, and I turn the page for him.

"Again."

He doesn't even question my reasons. I knew he wouldn't. After he places his last signature on the final page, he shoves it across the desk to me.

I look from the stack of papers and then back up at him. "Don't you even want to know why you signed your life away to me?" I ask.

He runs his hand down his face but doesn't answer. His blue eyes have turned black, and his jaw is tight. Now that he's not suffocating, he's quite angry that I just forced his hand. What is a life worth to you, sort of thing?

I look up at Bones. "Wouldn't you want to know why someone wanted you dead?"

"Absolutely," he answers.

"The only reason you wouldn't ask questions is if ... you already knew."

Still, he says nothing.

"Rossi has called you." I fish.

He flinches at the name. I smile. Yep. He's very well aware of why I'm here and what I want.

"Well, too bad for you, I'm not as forgiving as he is."

He goes to open his mouth, but I remove the knife from my pocket, flip it open, and stand, bringing it down on to the center of his hand, stabbing it to the desk.

He howls like a wolf as the blood instantly pools underneath it.

I toss the papers to the floor to keep them clean. "You made a deal with him. Before or after you made one with me?" I demand.

"Af ... ter," he cries out. His free hand grips the wrist of the hand pinned to his desk. "I didn't have a choice," he adds quickly.

"How much?" I demand, holding the pocketknife in place.

He's out of his seat, bent over the desk. Spit falls out of the corner of his lips and onto the surface. "One ... million."

"That had to have been a hard offer to pass up," I muse. "That's six million dollars in your pocket, and you didn't have to do anything for it."

"Please ... I ..."

Removing the knife from my other pocket, I flip it open and stab it through his other hand, pinning it to the desk as well.

He screams so loud, the shrill hurts my ears. "Please ..." he pleads, closing his eyes tightly, trying to hide his tears.

I look up at Bones and nod. He places the plastic bag back over his head. This time he pulls out a roll of duct tape from the duffel. He then proceeds to wrap the tape around his neck, securing the bag to his head.

I sit back in my seat and watch the fat bastard lean over his desk, fighting to breathe. To move.

"Listen to me," I order, but he's in panic mode, his body thrashing uncontrollably. I shoved the knives so far through his hands and into the desk that he won't be able to get free unless he wants to rip them in half.

Bones leans over his back and grabs his face on either side, forcing him to look up at me. "Pay attention," he orders.

"Did you know that it can take thirty seconds or thirty minutes to suffocate?" I ask. "It all depends on how much you fight it."

He struggles, and his voice muffled. His mouth gaping as the bag sticks to his face while he tries to breathe. It's wet from saliva and tears.

"Suffocation doesn't hurt. So I thought I'd add the pain." I wiggle the knives, and he bangs his hips into the desk, making the wooden legs scrape across the tile and objects fall off the sides to the floor. "And just to make sure you don't survive, I'm going to cut your head off before we bury you in the desert."

Blood covers his desk as Bones and I watch the man lose his life second by second. Within a few minutes, his face grows white. His lips purple. His fight turns to nothing. He face-plants into the blood, and all movement stops. I stand, buttoning up my suit jacket. "Take care of him. I want his head at least three miles from his rotting corpse," I order and then pick up the papers off the floor and exit his office. Bones doesn't usually take care of dead bodies. We pay people for that, but I know he has my back on this. I'll owe him, and when he calls, I'll pay up. No matter the price.

I go to walk down the hall when I see her mother exit a door at the end on the left. I make my way toward her.

"Luca? What are you doing here so late? I thought I heard …"

I slap a hand over her mouth and shove her back into the wall with so much force it knocks a picture off, sending it crashing to the floor and shattering at our feet. Her green eyes go wide with horror.

"I'm going to give you one chance. One chance to explain what you know. Do you understand me?"

She nods quickly.

I step away, and she sucks in a long breath. Tears streak her cheeks as her eyes go from mine to the office door.

"Rossi," I say, just in case we're not on the same page. "Did you know he went to your husband?"

"No." She gasps out. "Well, I did but not until after."

"Make sense," I grind out through gritted teeth.

"I overheard him talking in his study. He thought I was out shopping. He had Rossi on speakerphone. He told him the banks were in debt, and that he needed a loan. Rossi laughed. Then there was silence." She sucks in a deep breath. "I guessed he had hung up. That's when I reached out to you. I knew you'd do the right thing for her. She missed you so much, and I knew you could protect her. Then just a week ago, I overheard another conversation between them. Rossi had seen the pictures from the engagement party and wanted to know how much you paid him for Haven. That he'd double it. One million up front and the rest after it was done."

"After what was done?" I demand, but I already know the answer.

"Said all he had to do was give him the time and location of the wedding. That he didn't care if she was caught in the crossfire. That it would make him look good. Dead. Adopted daughter killed in a mass shooting at her own wedding. The press would eat it up."

Motherfucker! My jaw clenches. "Why didn't you come to me? Or her?" Anything would have been nice. I knew the risk the Mafia put my life in by the time I was eight. But Haven? I have to protect her no matter the cost.

"I tried to tell her at the spa, but your men interrupted us and took her away. She's avoided me. That was the first chance I had. I was afraid that he would find out that I knew his and Rossi's plan. I couldn't chance putting Haven's life in danger. Even now ..." She sniffs. "If he found out that you knew he betrayed you? I don't know what he would do to Haven." Her wide eyes dart around the empty hallway.

I grab her hand and pull her toward the office.

"Luca. What are you ...?"

I shove her into the office, and she gasps when she sees her husband bent over dead on the desk. He's facedown, hands still pinned to the surface with the two knives. Bones stands behind him with his cell to his ear. "Make it fifteen minutes," he orders and ends the call once he sees us.

"Oh my God." Her shaky hands come to her face to cover her mouth. "Is he ...?"

"Yes," I say simply. "He was willing to put her life in danger. I couldn't take that chance."

She spins around and buries her head into my chest. "Thank you." She begins to sob. "Thank you for saving her. I knew you would."

Awkwardly, I rub her back. "I'll give you five minutes."

She looks up at me, her green eyes swimming in tears. Her cheeks red and lips swollen. She looks nothing like Haven. No one would ever guess she is her biological mother. And as much as I hate this woman for lying to Haven all her life, I have to protect her. I can't let Rossi come after her too. "For what?"

"To pack a bag. You're coming with me."

SIXTEEN

HAVEN

"I DON'T BELIEVE you," I say, trying to keep the tears at bay, but it's pointless.

He gives me a sly smile that just twists the knife that is already piercing my heart. "Ask your mother. There is DNA evidence."

I shake my head. "No ..."

"How about you do one?" He opens his top drawer and pulls out a small baggie. Lifting his right hand, he pulls a piece of hair out of his head and places it in the bag before he zips it. "You can see for yourself." He slides it across the desk. "Don't say I never gave you anything."

My stomach drops, and the hairs on my arms stand. It feels like a million little bugs are crawling over my skin. "I want nothing from you," I whisper.

He gives a rough laugh. "Everyone wants something from me, Haven. Whether that be protection or money. And you are no exception."

"Why now?" I hear myself asking but can't find the courage to look up at him.

"Because you have something I want."

Closing my eyes, a tear runs down my cheek.

"Haven." His voice is soft yet firm and demands my attention.

I open my eyes and look up at him through watery lashes.

"No Rossi will marry a Bianchi."

His words are final. Like a nail in a coffin. The last breath taken. I will die, and it will be soon. I know what kind of man he is. I may not know him personally, but he's just like Luca and his family. They will take out who they want, and they don't care who stands in their way.

"I know you don't want to be with that bastard," he spits out, his hatred for Luca showing. "Daddy is going to take care of your problem. You have nothing to worry about."

I'M SITTING ON THE BALCONY OF OUR ROOM, SMOKING A cigarette. My hair still wet from my shower and up in a clippie. I have a pair of Luca's sweatpants and a T-shirt on. I don't know where he went, but I haven't cared enough to call or text him either.

So much has changed since this morning. Who I am? Where did I come from?

My father is Alberto Rossi. A mob boss who runs the South Side of Las Vegas. And I'm engaged to my ex, who just so happens to be his enemy.

My life is shit.

I take another drag from the cigarette and slowly blow out the smoke. Resting my head back, I hear the sliding glass door open.

Luca walks outside along with Nite and my mother. My jaw tightens at the look on her face. Her tear-streaked face. The proof she's been upset.

Fuck her.

She wasn't lied to all her life. Sentenced to death for loving the wrong man. In the end, we'll all have to answer to God for our sins, but mine will be for falling in love. Since when should you go to hell for that?

"Why is she here?" I ask him.

"Your mother needs to talk you." His answer is clipped. I'm not sure who he's mad at more—her or me—but at this point, I don't care.

I look at Nite. "Why is he here?" He's supposed to be protecting Mia.

"Your two newest bodyguards are being burned as we speak, so he's been assigned back to you."

My mother gasps. I take another puff of my cigarette. Wonder if they were dead or alive when their bodies were set on fire?

"Haven?" She sucks in a long breath. "Since when did you start smoking?"

I can't help it. I throw my head back laughing. Out of all the things that have happened in the past twenty-four hours, that's what she wants to focus on.

"You need to talk to your mother," Luca says.

I look up at him. Now he wants me to be social? "She lied to me all my life. Why would I listen to her now?"

She sits down beside me and reaches out for my hand, but I jerk it out of her reach.

"I had to protect you," she whispers.

I snort and take a drag of the cigarette.

"Haven ...?"

"Was any of it true?" I snap, unable to keep it in. I threw that stupid piece of hair away, but a part of me knew he was right. I just can't understand why she wouldn't tell me. I thought we were close.

She bows her head. "No."

I lean forward in my seat. "Start from the beginning," I demand, needing to know. When she stays silent, I help her out. "The miscarriages?"

"A lie," she whispers.

Unbelievable. "Who the fuck lies about that?"

"You wouldn't understand," she whispers.

"Try me," I snap.

She takes in a deep breath, and her shoulders fall. "Your grandfather ... he wanted grandchildren. He wanted your father to have an heir."

There's that word again. *Heir*. "This is bullshit." I stand.

"Haven." She reaches up and grabs my wrist. "I ... please sit." Her eyes plead with me to give her a chance, to forgive her, but I'm not sure I can. No matter what she tells me, I'm not sure I can give her what she wants right now. "I'm begging you. Please. Just listen to the truth. I'll leave afterward," she assures me.

I look at Luca for help—reassurance that he will kick her out once she finally gives me what I should have known all along—but I don't get the answer I want. He feels sorry for her. I can see it in his dark eyes. And pity for me. I hate it. Letting out a long breath, I plop back down into the chair next to her.

"Your father and I had an arranged marriage. He didn't love me. I didn't love him. The wedding was to forge two businesses as one. I felt lonely. He would never touch me, never look at me. He had different women over all the time. His father was pressuring us to have a family." She swallows. "One night, I went out to a bar and got drunk. I met the owner, who just happened to be a guy I had seen around your father. He had been to our house before."

I know who she's talking about. Alberto Rossi. "They were friends?"

She gives a rough laugh and plucks the lit cigarette from my hand, taking a drag. My eyes widen. "I wouldn't call them that. They did business together. He used your father's bank to launder money."

I look at Luca, and he runs a hand through his hair aggressively.

"Then what happened?" I ask.

She gives a wistful smile. "He treated me how my husband was supposed to, and I fell in love."

Silence falls over the balcony. I look back up at Luca, and he turns, giving us his back as he looks out over Las Vegas, but his white-knuckled grip on the railing tells me he's pissed. Nite stands over in the corner with his arms crossed over his chest, silently listening to us.

I shift in my seat and look back at my mom. "I don't understand."

"I opened up to him, and he let me cry on his shoulder. I found myself going back to that bar night after night just to see him. I just wanted to talk to him, but then one thing led to another. He told me all the right things. Three months later, I found out I was pregnant. I went to his bar and told him the news. I was going to have his baby, and I wanted to leave my useless husband." She shakes her head. "It was all a lie."

"How?" *A lie?*

"It was a setup. Rossi informed me that Jimmy knew I was sleeping with him. He told him to knock me up, so he wouldn't have to do it."

I jump to my feet. "They what?" I yell. "He told Rossi to fuck you? His wife?" I seethe, not understanding. Yes, my parents have had their arguments, but I've never seen them not in love. Was all that a lie too? For me? For my grandfather? He passed years ago. Why continue with the ruse if they no longer needed to fake it?

She looks up at me, tears filling her eyes. "You need to understand. Your grandfather was pressuring him to produce a child. He needed me ..."

"He played you," I growl.

She bows her head and shakes it. "I can't ... I can't hate him for what he did."

"Why the hell not?" I snap.

She looks up at me and stands. Gripping my hands, they shake in mine. "Because I got you, Haven. You were everything I ever wanted."

My heart pounds at her words.

"Your father and I decided to tell you that you were adopted."

"The papers? You have adoption papers that you keep in the safe. I've seen them."

She gives me a sad smile. "Fake."

I take a step back from her, and my hands drop to my sides. "Why?"

"You father and Rossi had a deal ..."

"Jimmy is not my father!" I shout.

She wraps her arms around herself. "He and Rossi cut all ties. Rossi paid him cash to pretend you were adopted, and we came up with that story. But please, Haven ... please believe that you were always wanted. We wanted you from the moment we found out I was pregnant."

I snort. "Of course, he was. He had his friend knock you up. On purpose. To make his dad happy," I snap, disgusted but somehow not surprised.

"But Rossi couldn't stay away." Luca finally speaks.

My mother turns to him, and she swallows nervously. "He did for a while. But... he—"

"He what?" Luca demands, taking a step toward her. "Why did he come back into her life twenty-four years later? I can't seem to stop asking myself this question. We dated years before our engagement party, and it wasn't any secret. The media has always been in my life. And pictures have surfaced in the past with Haven on my arm. Why does he care now?"

"Rossi called me a couple of years back. Said he heard she was dating a Bianchi and for me to forbid it. I lied, told him it was harmless, and that it would fizzle out. Just to give it time. But ..." She pauses and looks over at Nite who still stands like a statue over in the corner. "He wanted to get Luca away from you." Tears run down her cheeks.

"What did he do?" I demand and look at Luca. "I don't under ..." But one look at him lets me know he does. Perfectly.

He takes a step toward my mother, hands fisted and eyes now black as the night. "He set me up too," he growls.

She sniffs. "You have to understand. There was nothing I could have done. He and my husband agreed. I had no say."

"Bullshit!" he snaps.

Why am I the only one lost? "Luca—"

"I had to keep her safe," my mother wails, interrupting me.

"I could have kept her safe!" he shouts. "You should have come to me. Been honest."

"You're in the Mafia!" she shouts back at him. "I know what you're capable of. And how much your father hated you two together." She shoves his chest, but he doesn't move. Fresh tears run down her face, and she looks at Nite. "At the time, I felt helpless. My hands were tied, and I couldn't lose her. Luca couldn't have run forever. If his father wouldn't have found him, Rossi would have."

I look back at Luca, confused. Why is she talking to Nite?

"I couldn't stop what had already been done," she goes on.

"What had been done?" I ask.

Everyone turns to me, but Luca is the one who speaks. "Rossi set me up. He kidnapped Nite and tortured him to talk about Mia. He knew she existed because he and my father were friends when she was born. He had threatened her life. But ..."

"But what?" I ask breathlessly. My chest already tight.

"He knew I would run to her to protect her. But he was never going to touch her." He shakes his head, his jaw sharpening. "No. He did it to get me away from you."

My eyes slam to Nite. "No," I whisper. It wasn't Mia's fault. She didn't do that to him. It was me. "Oh, God." I fall into the seat, but no one pays me any attention.

"Do you have any idea how hard I tried to find something you could use against him?" my mother asks Luca. "How I put my life in danger every day snooping around trying to find you some leverage?"

"And why was that, Misty?" he snaps.

"Because you leaving ripped my daughter apart!" she shouts in his face. "She loved you. She needed you. And I know you loved her too."

He runs a hand through his hair. "Un-fucking-believable. Do you have any idea what kind of danger you put her life in?" he growls. "How me leaving left her wide open? A target? I thought ... I thought I was doing the right thing by leaving her," he continues.

"If you would have known the truth, you would have

acted. Thought irrationally. I just needed some time. I knew where you went. You hadn't run off with another woman. You were just trying to protect your sister. And I knew once I had the info I needed, you'd come running back to her."

How does my mother know about Mia? I thought she was kept a secret. How ... my chest aches. I hurt Nite. I was never friends with the guy, but he was used as bait because of me. They were all tricked because of me.

"I'm sorry." I stand, looking at Nite with tears running down my face. "I'm so sorry, Nite. I don't expect you to forgive me. But I hate that I hurt you. I hate that Rossi used you." My voice breaks. "I'm so, so sorry."

His eyes cut to Luca, and he nods once.

"We'll leave you two alone for a second." My mother looks like she's about to argue, but Luca grabs her arm and drags her back into our bedroom, closing the sliding glass door behind them.

"I'm so sorry. I wish I would have known. I would have ..."

"I forgive you."

My eyes widen, and my lips part on a gasp. I stare up at him in shock as he kneels in front of me. Placing his hands on my shaking knees, he repeats, "I forgive you, Haven. Do you understand? It wasn't your fault." His voice is deep and rough but in a soothing way.

My wide eyes go back and forth between his. "You spoke," I choke out.

He nods.

"Say something," I demand, placing my hands on his broad shoulders, gripping them tightly, wanting to hear it again. I didn't imagine it.

"I said I forgive you."

"But ... but they cut your tongue out." I can't help but

blurt out. "Because of me. Because..." My bottom lip quivers.

He gives me a cocky smile that lights up his face. Oliver Nite never smiles. Not even before ...

He sticks his tongue out, and my eyes widen even more if possible. "There's a difference in being unable to talk and choosing not to."

"But ... what ... how?" My brain can't comprehend what I'm hearing. All this time? Why is he pretending to be a mute? And what is he gaining from it?

"Another time," he says, standing. Grabbing my hands, he pulls me to my feet. "Just know that I never blamed Mia. And I'm not going to blame you either. We all make our own choices, Haven. And I'm living with mine just fine." Then he turns and walks back into the bedroom as well.

I go barging in to find all three of them standing in the middle of our bedroom. My mother and Luca are still arguing. Nite stands there with his arms crossed over his chest, looking like he didn't just speak to me. He didn't have to tell me to keep what just took place between us. A part of me knows that Luca knew exactly what was going to happen, and that's why he ushered my mother from the balcony. But whatever that was between me and Nite is now over. He's back to Silent Nite. And I will keep his secret.

"My ..." I clear my throat. "Jimmy?" I ask. "How do we know he won't double-cross us again?" I ask. I've received so much info in such little time. I need to prioritize it and figure out my biggest threat. He's far up on the list.

Their bickering comes to a halt, and they all turn to look at me.

"You don't have to worry about that," Luca assures me.

"He killed him," my mother answers.

"What?" My wide eyes go to Luca.

His jaw sharpens as he glares down at my mom.

"I won't tell her another lie." She glares back up at him. "Or hide anything from her. He's dead. The end."

"I ... did he hurt you?" I ask Luca.

He comes over to me and grips my hands in his. "No. He was going to sit back and let your life be ruined for fucking cash in his pocket. He deserved death."

"So ..." I swallow nervously and remove the clip from my wet hair. It falls down over my shoulders, instantly soaking the shirt I'm wearing. "What do we do?" I ask, trying to figure out how I'm going to use all this information.

The man I've called my father all my life is dead. My biological father can't be beat, or he would already be dead. I'm not sure how this can end well for any of us.

"We go to Kingdom. Pack a bag," Luca orders.

"It's almost two a.m.," I say, wondering why in the hell we're going there.

LUCA

REMOVING MY SUIT jacket, I lay it across the back of the couch in our hotel suite on the thirtieth floor at Kingdom. Her mom goes over to the sliding glass door, opens it, and steps outside for fresh air. Haven follows her.

I turn to Bones and Titan. "Thank you."

Bones nods. "You know you are welcome here anytime."

Titan crosses his arms over his chest and adjusts his stance, widening his legs. "We've got two guards standing outside of your room and snipers on the roof ..."

"Why do we need snipers?" Haven asks, re-entering the suite.

"Safety," I answer.

"Luca. What are you not telling me?" She looks around the room. "Why are we here at Kingdom and not at home?"

I want to feel happy that she referred to my house as our home, but I don't have the time. I run a hand through my hair. "He doesn't plan to let you live." Her eyes widen. "Rossi is planning on taking more out than just me and the Kings at the ceremony."

"What? No. He told me—"

"He lied," I interrupt her. "You think he'd protect you? He never wanted you. He hates us." I point at my chest. "You're marrying the enemy. Either you die as collateral damage or are killed on purpose. I'm not taking that chance. There is better protection here. The numbers are bigger." Plus, Rossi won't step foot near Kingdom. He may want the Dark Kings dead as well, but he wouldn't do it on their territory. He's too much of a coward. He knows he's outnumbered here. We just took out more of his men, so he will have to regroup and think of a new plan. And we'll already be executing ours.

She bows her head, running her hand through her hair. "What if ...?" She bites her lip in thought. "What if we get married now? Go to the courthouse and get it over with as soon as they open? Will that make a difference? Isn't there some unwritten rule about going after a Mafia wife?" She rolls her sleepy eyes at that. "Not saying it's still not done, but he may think twice if he knows the consequences are worse."

Her mother steps into the room and five sets of eyes stare at her. "What?" she asks, looking around at all of us.

I step forward. "We're already married."

"Luca, this isn't the time to ..." Her words trail off, and her eyes go big. "What?" she whispers. Recognition dawns on her face, and she places her hand on her head. "The contract ... it was a marriage license?" Her eyes narrow on me. "I didn't sign anything."

I take another step. "Your name is on it. Whether you signed it is not the point." On paper, she is my wife.

She tilts her head to the side, tears building in her eyes. "You tricked me."

I say nothing.

She looks around the room. "And you all knew."

Again, no one speaks because they all did. Even her mother.

"Mom?" She turns to face her. "You knew this?"

She nods softly. "I had to ..."

"How could you?" Her voice cracks.

"I told you at the clubhouse. You needed to be a Bianchi—"

"No," she interrupts her. "You could have told me. You could have ..."

"I couldn't say anything. It would have cost you your life!" she shouts, getting angry. "Why can't you get this through your head? You know what kind of weight has been on my shoulders ever since I got pregnant with you?" she screams. "Haven." She lowers her voice and walks over to her. Grabbing her hands, she continues, "I prayed every day that he wouldn't want you. Even after he allowed your father to adopt you, I still feared he'd come for you." Her eyes go to mine before returning to her daughter. "I needed Luca to save you. He was the only one who could. So I did what was best for you."

She rips her hands from her mother's and turns to face me. "So, what? The wedding was just going to be a formality?"

"Yes," I say simply.

She looks at Bones then at Titan, but they stay quiet.

This isn't their fight. They may have known my plans, but their loyalty is to me. Not her.

Her brows pull together in deep thought, and then her brown eyes fill with fresh tears as she looks up at me. "Did you know he was my father?" I open my mouth, but she continues. "Is this why you did this? Picked me?"

"Haven ...?"

"Your family has been fighting with Rossi for years. This would be the ultimate *fuck you*. Marrying his daughter and posting it for the world to see. Rubbing it in his face."

I take the three steps to close the small distance. Placing both of my hands on her tear-streaked face, I cup her cheeks. "No. You know this." She's already asked me this once. "I've always loved you, Haven. You are a Bianchi now. And I will protect you until I die. If that means lying to you, then that's what I will do."

She pulls away from me, and my hands fall to my sides. Then, without another word, she turns and enters the master suite.

"Haven ..." her mother calls out, following her.

She slams the door in her face, and the sound of the lock follows.

SEVENTEEN

HAVEN

I PACE BACK and forth in the bedroom. My arms crossed over my chest and tears in my eyes.

I'm married.

I'm fucking married.

No matter how many times I repeat it, I can't believe it.

He tricked me. That part isn't so hard to comprehend. That's a Bianchi for you. I knew he was keeping something from me.

"Fucking liar," I growl, fisting my hands.

Was he ever going to tell me? I don't remember the contract mentioning marriage exactly. Just children. I need to read it. What else is on there?

Storming out of the bedroom, I come to a stop when I see the suite is empty. I look around the open living room and kitchen. There's a door on the other side of the living room, but it's open. It must be to another bedroom. "Mom?" I call out. *Nothing.* "Luca?" I demand. *Nothing.*

I walk across the living room and pass the bar, entering the kitchen. I yank open the fridge and grab a bottle of water. Turning around, I jump when I see Nite standing in

209

the living room with his arms crossed over his chest. "Jesus." I hiss. "Where the hell did Luca go?"

He doesn't answer.

My teeth grind. "So, we're back to this?"

Still, he says nothing. I want to be mad at him, but I can't. I hate what I did to him. What Rossi did to him. "I'm sorry," I say softly. He showed me something very personal, and I don't want him to think he owes me. If anything, I owe him.

"Did Luca leave with Bones and Titan?"

He nods, which means they're in the hotel somewhere. Probably meeting with the others to go over their plan.

"Did my mother get her own room?" I ask.

He nods again.

I figured she would. Leaving him standing in the living room, I re-enter the bedroom and unzip my Louis Vuitton suitcase and remove my phone. I call Em. Even after everything that has been going on with me, I think of her all the time. When it rings, my heart soars, thinking that this may be the time I get to hear her voice. I miss her so much. I could really use her right now. But it drops when I get her voicemail after the third ring. "Hey, you've reached Emilee. I'm not available at this time ..."

I hang up and flop onto the bed. Closing my eyes, I take a deep breath as a tear runs down the side of my cheek. I open them up, roll over to my stomach, and hit call on the next number.

"What up, sexy?" Jasmine asks on the first ring. I can always count on her.

"Are you busy?" I ask, trying not to lose my shit. I want to cry. I want to scream. I just want to not feel trapped. I should be afraid of Rossi, but I'm madder at Luca than anything. And I know that's not fair. He's just trying to protect me, even if he's doing it wrong.

"Nope. What's up?"

"Wanna meet me at Kingdom?" I ask, wiping the tears from my face and sit up.

"Sure. In the mood to gamble?"

"No. I wanna drink."

KINGDOM IS MORE THAN A CASINO. IT'S A SMALL CITY all on its own. You can walk into the buildings and never leave. It has over ten restaurants. Three night clubs. Twenty sports bars. A tattoo shop. A shopping mall that connects all four towers. Golf course, bowling alley, wedding chapel, five pools, and its own theater with ten screens. They play movies twenty-four seven. And not to mention the largest convention center. It sponsors anything from UFC fights to sold-out concerts. There's talk that next year's CMAs will be held there.

You want it, Kingdom supplies it. The Dark Kings made sure to offer their gamblers anything and everything. All you gotta do is have the money, and it's yours. They want you to come and never have to leave.

My favorite place is Crown, one of their nightclubs.

Jasmine looks over her shoulder. "I'm serious, Nite. That offer still stands." She licks her lips.

I roll my eyes and turn her back to watch where she's going. I wanted to drink in our suite. It was stocked with a full bar and has plenty of liquid to get us both wasted, but she wanted to go out. It didn't take much for me to give in. But of course, Nite had to follow. He's back on babysitting duty since his return. Especially now that Rossi is after Luca.

"Is he going to follow us all night?" Jasmine yells in my ear, looking at him over her shoulder.

"Most likely," I answer, walking up to the bar and sitting on a stool. Jasmine plops down beside me. Looking over the shelf of alcohol behind it, she smiles when she decides what she wants. "Two shots of Patrón," she calls out to no one in particular. Two bartenders scurry around to make drinks but neither one has waited on us yet.

"Porn Star Dancing" by My Darkest Day blares in the club.

I look over at her, arching a brow.

"You never got a bachelorette party, so this is it."

I had told her about my marriage while in the elevator. She didn't seem to care as much as I did that I'm already married. Or that my father was dead and my biological father plans on killing me. I had a lot to get out in a short amount of time. It was like vomit. A sickness that I needed to purge even though I don't feel any better. Of course, she wants us to party. Em would try to talk it out, to help me understand it all and see the bright side of where my life is headed, but Jasmine just wants to pour alcohol down my throat. And as I sit here at the bar under the neon flashing lights and pounding music, I realize she's right. I need to drown it out. Bury it. There's nothing I can do about the situation. I'm a wife. A Mafia wife. Till death do us part.

A mob boss who just so happens to be my father wants me dead. There's a target on my husband's head. How much has Rossi offered to have him killed?

And it makes me feel stupid. He could have killed me when I met with him. The only reason he didn't was because he wants Luca. He thinks he can use me. Every man in my life thinks I'm just a pawn in their game. Well, fuck them.

Just then I spot a man who walks through the club and steps behind the bar. He leans down and tells the female bartender something. She nods a few times. As he goes to exit from behind the bar, I call out to him. "Grave?"

He turns back to face the bar and smiles when his eyes meet mine. "Haven?" He walks over to us. Placing his forearms on the bar, he leans over it. "What are you doing here?" Grave has the cutest baby face. With his blue eyes and perfect smile, he's also the most approachable of the Kings. He's covered in just as many tats as the others and has a piercing in his brow, but he has a kind soul. But just like the others, he has his demons to fight. "Where's Luca?"

I shrug. "Somewhere with your brother."

He smiles. "I see." And then he straightens. "What can I get you lovely ladies?"

"Two shots of Patrón."

LUCA

Nite: We're at Crown.

I read the message that Nite sends me.

Me: Stay with her.

I respond before placing my phone back in my pocket.

"Thanks," Bones says into his cell and places it on his desk, leaning back in his chair. "My source says he's not in Vegas."

"Well, he was," Titan says, sitting in the chair next to me. "And he'll be back." He looks over at me. "Your *wedding*"—he makes air quotes— "is days away. He will want to do the job himself."

I rub my chin in thought. "Yeah, but we can't let him get that close. I don't want Haven anywhere near that situation. But I can't call off the ceremony. That will be suspicious. Throw up too many red flags."

"You need to publicly make the current venue unavailable," Bones suggests.

Not a bad idea. "I'm listening."

He sits up straighter. "Force him to go where you want him to. We will be ready for him. You could even have it here if you want. We can arrange for snipers on the roof of Kingdom. They'll be able to see him and his men a mile away. Not to mention he won't be able to turn the opportunity down since he wants us too."

"He knows we'll be at the wedding no matter where it's held," Titan argues.

"Yes, but this gives him an advantage," Bones says.

"How?" Titan asks.

"By letting him think he can kill us on our own turf." He shrugs. "Rossi is a cocky son of a bitch. And to take us all out on Kingdom property ...? He'll be drooling at the chance."

"It could work," I say. "But Haven ..."

"Won't even be here," Bones adds.

"Where will she be?" Titan asks the same thing I'm thinking.

"She'll be at our compound with our security."

"I want Nite with her," I say, thinking about my options.

"Whoever you want." Bones nods.

"He'll want to fight with you," Titan adds. "He's loyal to you."

"Then he will do what I tell him to," I growl, knowing

he's right. I want him with Haven. There are only five guys I trust with my life who are not blood related, and Nite is number fucking one. Two of the other four are currently in this room.

"I don't know," Titan speaks. "It could still tip him off. He pulls Haven away from you to speak to her. Then his men go missing. Now you want to take the one location he plans on killing us out of the game?" He shakes his head. "He could get spooked. Think she informed you of his plan. What are the odds that someone else besides her knows his plan?"

Bones smiles. "He'll get nervous. And men who are nervous will fuck up."

I stand, making up my mind. "I need to talk to Cross."

EIGHTEEN
HAVEN

I STUMBLE OUT of the elevator laughing. Jasmine has her arm hooked through mine and her free hand on the wall to help stabilize us.

We had a lot to drink at the club. Grave hooked us up. The shots just kept coming, and we kept swallowing them.

I see the two guys standing guard outside our hotel suite. They look at Nite, and he nods once. I'm sure it's some code for we're all right. Just two wasted women who can't hold their liquor. Jasmine already puked twice in the bathroom, then she washed her mouth out with a shot of vodka. I threw up once in the bathroom sink.

Good times.

We come up to the door. She tries to push the door open, but it doesn't budge. Leaning forward, she places her face to the door and cups her lips. "Please open up."

"What the hell are you doing?" I ask with a laugh.

"Communication is key," she slurs.

I shove her out of the way so hard she falls onto her ass. "You had way too many cocktails," I say, but my laughter grows.

"I haven't had any cock yet tonight." She looks up at Nite. "How about—"

"Stop it," I interrupt her. *Poor Nite.* He probably hates Luca for putting him on babysitting duty. I want to ask why he isn't with Mia anymore but stop myself before I do. This is not the place, and Jasmine may be my best friend, but no one is supposed to know that Mia exists. Plus, he wouldn't answer me anyway.

"I'm gonna give up alcohol," she states, sitting up to place her back against the black and gold wallpaper of the hallway.

I snort and dig through my purse for the hotel key. I hope I grabbed it.

"I'm going to do sober October."

I look down to see Nite grab her arms and lift her drunken body up off the floor. "It's May," I inform her.

She shrugs awkwardly. "And no sex November."

"Dear Lord ..."

"No dick December. No fuck February."

"You skipped over January."

"Why is it so hard to find good dick?" she asks, ignoring me. "Like I don't wanna be loved." She laughs. "I just want someone who will lick my pussy and fuck my ass." She spins around, her hands slapping Nite. She looks up at him with her heavy eyes. "I bet you know how to fuck a woman." She reaches out to grab his crotch, but he moves quickly, capturing her wrists and holding them away from him. "The silent and brooding ones are always the dirtiest."

The door yanks open, and I turn to see Luca. It's three a.m., and he stands there dressed in a button-down and slacks. "Why are you standing out here?" he demands.

"I couldn't find my key." I hiccup, not sure why Nite

didn't use his. Maybe he was enjoying the show that Jasmine was giving him.

"Trying to get laid." Jasmine smiles.

He steps to the side and gestures for us to enter. Jasmine trips into the room, and Nite reaches for her and keeps her standing. Her knees buckle, and he slides one hand behind her back and the other underneath her knees and picks her up. Her head falls back over his arm, and she closes her heavy eyes.

Luca sighs as Nite walks through the door and takes her over to the guest room off the side of the kitchen.

"I guess you had fun?" he asks me, closing the door.

I ignore him and head to our bedroom. I trip over my heels and silently curse myself.

"Haven, I'm talking to you," he growls.

I snort.

"Haven?" He grips my upper arm and pulls me to a stop. I spin around to yell at him, but words die on my tongue as I catch sight of the TV that hangs on the living room wall.

It's the local news channel. A woman stands outside of a cathedral. The cathedral we plan on getting married at next week. It's gone. "What ...?" I stumble away from him, and he releases me. I fall onto the cream leather couch in the living room and watch as the reporter explains there had been a fire. St. Mary's Cathedral is a complete loss, but thankfully, the place was empty. "At this time, some are throwing speculation out regarding arson, but nothing has been confirmed yet ..." The reporter goes on. "The fire marshal ..."

"We were going to get married there," I say, turning to look over my shoulder at Luca.

He stands behind the couch with his arms crossed over

219

his chest. His dark eyes are focused on mine. He doesn't seem the least bit concerned. Or surprised.

My heart begins to pound as I stand on shaky legs. I turn my body fully so I can face him. "Did you do this?" I ask.

He just stares at me.

"Luca." I lick my numb lips. "Why?" I ask. He doesn't have to admit it out loud because I know he's responsible.

"We needed to change the venue."

"What?" I ask, cupping my forehead. The room is starting to spin, and my eyes are heavy. I'm either going to get sick or pass out very soon. "Why ...?"

"We need to bring Rossi to us. And we needed to do it without tipping him off that we're onto his plan. He can't know that you are on our side."

"So you burn down a place of worship?" I ask in horror. "Dear Lord, it's like college all over again. When Cross ..." I pause as my words sink into my foggy brain. I look to my right where he stands there next to Bones. "You had Cross do it," I say breathlessly, falling back down onto the couch.

Cross got his name in grade school. He had marks all over his back that looked like crosses. We could only guess where he got them from. And we all came to the same conclusion. His father. But Cross got his revenge. He doesn't carry around a Zippo for nothing. He likes fire. The heat of the flames. He'll burn you with no remorse.

I begin to rock back and forth. "It'll never work," I say even though I don't know his plan. The Dark Kings obviously had a hand in it as well. Rossi will take them all out. He's too smart. Too protected. They're going to serve themselves up on a silver platter.

"Haven ..."

"Not to mention the fire marshal ... They are going to

investigate," I continue blabbering. "He'll get caught. Arson ..."

"Haven!"

Hands grip my shoulder, and then I'm being shaken.

My heavy eyes land on Luca's as he kneels before me. "Calm down. You're drunk and overreacting. Trust me, I have it all handled."

"And if you don't?" I can't help but ask. I'm still mad at him, but that doesn't mean I want us all to die. All I've ever wanted was him. I look down at my ring. I thought I still had time to escape this wedding, this life, but the joke is on me. I'm already in it. Then I wonder if I had a chance to get out, would I? I'm not sure. I've always loved Luca. What if I lose him now? It would hurt too much.

"I do," he says simply.

LUCA

I TUCK A very drunk Haven into our bed. She passed out right after I managed to calm her down. She was on the verge of hysterics. I know she's scared, but she was also unable to think rationally. Alcohol will do that to you.

Exiting our bedroom, I see Cross standing in the living room. He's staring at the TV. They are still reporting on the church fire, which is good. I needed it to make the headlines.

Another man I know well stands next to him with his hands in the front pockets of his slacks. He too watches the news.

"Jeffrey," I say, getting their attention. "Glad you were able to meet with me on such short notice." I look over at the open kitchen to see Grave making some drinks. Titan sits on the couch and Bones leans up against the sliding glass door that leads to the balcony. My eyes go back to Jeffrey. "You know the drill," I tell him.

He sighs but starts to unbutton his black button-down. Once he gets to the last one, he opens his shirt to showcase a hairy chest and beer belly. Then he allows the shirt to drop off his shoulders, and he spins around, showing me his back.

I nod my approval.

He begins to button it back up. "I'm aware of what you need, Luca. You didn't need to send your dogs to retrieve me in the middle of the night."

Cross's brows pull together at that statement. Grave just laughs as he pours two more glasses of scotch.

"They're not my dogs," I say, referring to the Kings. I would have sent Nite, but I'm not removing him from Haven. He is to be with her at all times until Rossi is dead. "And you know I don't do business over the phone." Wires can be tapped. You never know who may be listening. And that's exactly why I made him undo his shirt and show me his chest. That day my father killed my uncle, I learned a lot about betrayal. It can come from anyone at any time. Always check before you open your mouth.

I walk over to the bar and pick up two of the drinks that Grave places on the counter. I walk back into the open living room and hand one to Jeffrey. Taking a sip of mine, I sit on the couch. "I expect you can handle it?" I question.

"Of course." He sounds offended. "A warning would have been nice, but I can take care of it."

"We didn't have much time to work with," Cross says, taking a full glass from Grave as he enters the living room as well.

Jeffrey throws back his drink. "How much evidence did you leave me?" He looks at Cross.

A slow smile spreads across his face. "Like I said, I

didn't have much time. Open oxygen tanks in the boiler room ..."

He hangs his head, running his hand through his hair. He looks back up at us just as his cell rings in his pocket. He digs it out and places it to his ear. "Hello ... Yeah, I'll be there in twenty." He hangs up.

I take a sip and call out. "Nite?"

He sits on the couch across from me. Standing, he places a black duffel bag on the glass coffee table. "It's all there," I tell Jeffrey. "You're free to count it."

He shakes his head. "I know you're good for it."

My father has had the fire marshal on our payroll for years now. Along with many other important people in this city. When you want to run a city, you have to own every inch of it. And we do. Whoever I don't own, the Kings do. We use each other's resources all the time.

"I hope you have a damn good reason for burning a cathedral to the ground," he says, eyeing us.

I arch a brow, a smile spreading across my face. "Afraid for our souls, Jeffrey?"

He shakes his head and sighs heavily. "I'm afraid for all of our souls, Bianchi."

"It's not like anything we do is forgivable," Titan adds.

With that, Jeffrey grabs the duffel bag and sees himself out.

Sitting back on the couch, I take a sip of the drink, feeling a little better about our situation. Now all we have to do is come up with a new plan to accommodate our new location.

NINETEEN

HAVEN

I SIT ON the couch in our hotel suite. Jasmine sits to my right. And we both stare up at the TV. Luca is walking out of Kingdom. He is dressed to impress with a charcoal gray three-piece suit on. His hair is slicked back, and his hands are in the pockets of his slacks. He walked out of our suite this morning, telling me he had to go to Glass. I know it was a lie. He needed to be seen. It's been three days since he put my drunk ass to sleep and we've been hiding out. I thought the news crew parked outside would give up and go away, but he knew better. The longer they waited, the sweeter this would be for him. The fire is on every news channel and the radio. It's all I hear people talking about when I walk through the casino. Not to mention social media. I've stayed off it, but Jasmine keeps sending me all these links.

News crews surround him. "What do you have to say about the burning of the cathedral?" one female reporter asks.

"Do you believe it's a sign from God to not marry?" another chimes in.

"You ever realize how stupid these damn questions are that the reporters ask?" Jasmine asks, shoving popcorn into her mouth.

"Yep," I answer.

Luca comes to a stop, slowly pushes his black shades to the top of his head. All chatter stops but the flashes from their cameras continue. He looks at the camera in his face and speaks. "What happened at St. Mary's Cathedral was a terrible loss. That's why I'm going to have it rebuilt." The people who surround him ahh and gasp at his generosity.

"Oh, he's good." Jasmine chuckles.

"Yeah, he is." I sigh.

The reporters start yelling, but he raises his hand to stop them. They silence at once. "And my wedding to the lovely Haven Knowles is still on. A fire isn't going to stop me from making her my wife."

I turn off the TV.

"Hey, I was watching that," Jasmine protests.

I stand from the couch and begin to pace. "He's making a point."

"To Rossi," she adds.

"That he's changed the location." The fire was ruled an accident.

The cathedral was old and needed updates. I guess they had had an inspection six months ago and were told that things needed to be replaced.

Such bullshit!

I know it. Luca knows it, and the Kings know it. Nothing would have caused an explosion that big at that time of night. I could see them saying a lit candle set the drapes on fire. Blah. Blah. Blah. But an explosion that brought down such a large portion of that big of a building in such a short time?

They paid someone off. That's the only situation that makes sense. I haven't brought it up and neither has he. He's been MIA for the most part. If he's not at Glass, he's here meeting with the Kings. I'm getting restless. It's supposed to be our wedding day. Well, our fake one.

Nite is here with me, but Luca said he wouldn't be back until later tonight and not to wait up for him. No one has filled me in with their new plan or location for the ceremony. No surprise there.

I do know that they plan on shipping my mother away. For protection, she had said. Just in case shit goes sideways, they wanted her protected.

I didn't argue. At this point, I just want us all to survive.

I overheard Luca telling Nite that the jet was fueled and waiting for us in case things don't go how he plans. I guess he's going to ship me off to Italy with Mia if Rossi wins.

I've prayed nonstop that he doesn't. But I highly doubt God is listening to me after my husband burned down a cathedral. We can hope.

"It's going to be okay," Jasmine speaks, getting through the fog.

I come to a stop and stare down at her. Tears filling my eyes. "And if it's not?" I can't help but ask.

She stands and walks over to me. "Then we'll leave together." She gives me a soft smile. "We're ride or die bitches. You go, and I go."

I open my mouth to argue with her, but my cell begins to ring on the coffee table. I pick it up, and my heart speeds up.

"Who is that?" she asks as I just stand staring down at it.

"Blocked number." I swallow.

"Answer it," she insists.

I shake my head. "I can't ..."

"Haven." She takes it from my hand. "If it's who we think it is, you need to talk to him. What if he suspects this happened on purpose, and he just watched Luca on TV? We need him to tell you his plan. To protect Luca, Nite, your mother, and the Kings. All involved."

"You're right." I nod. He's not only my father but also a very powerful man. I need to be ahead of the game. For others' sake. I quickly look around the massive suite. "Where is Nite?" I don't want him to hear this.

"He's in the shower."

"Answer it," I tell her.

She slides her finger across the screen before it stops ringing and puts it on speakerphone.

I clear my throat and try to sound like I'm not a scared little bitch. "Hello?"

"Hello, daughter."

I cringe at the word. "Rossi."

"I just saw Bianchi on the news. Terrible thing that happened to the cathedral."

I rub my sweaty hands down my thighs. "Yeah."

"You must be happy."

I frown, confused by what he means. "Happy?"

"Why, yes. Your wedding is postponed."

"Oh, yes. Very much so." I forgot that he thinks I hate Luca. That I don't want this wedding any more than he does.

"I'm sending a car."

What? My wide eyes go to Jasmine. "No, I—"

"I will see you in one hour," he interrupts me. "My driver will be outside of Kingdom for you. Don't make him wait."

"Rossi, I can't."

228

"Yes, you can. Your mother's life depends on it." *Click.*

She throws the phone onto the couch.

"Fuck!" I hiss. "My mother? What does that mean?" I grab my phone and call her cell. It goes straight to voice-mail. "Shit. Shit."

"When was the last time you spoke to her?" Jasmine asks, looking around the room aimlessly as if she will appear.

"I don't know. This morning. She was going down to the casino ..." I trail off. I never thought about her not returning. I thought maybe she stopped and was playing a machine. Or went to the spa. I don't keep track of her 24/7. "Oh, my God." I breathe. "He's taken her."

"We need Nite ..." She goes to leave the living room, but I grab her arm and stop her.

"No. Don't get him involved."

"Haven. This is serious. You're going to need help," she snaps, pushing her red hair behind her ear.

I run my hands through mine. "If he knows I got help, he may kill her. I can't take that chance."

She places both hands on my shoulders. "There's a possibility she's already dead. You can't take that chance."

I pull away and shake my head, unable to believe that scenario. "He wants me. Luca. He won't hurt her."

"You don't know that!" she shouts. "You're in this position because she went to Luca. What if he knows that?"

"Keep your voice down." I look around quickly to make sure Nite is still in the bathroom.

Her eyes narrow on me. "He's going to use you as bait. Make Luca go to him."

I know. Fucking bastard.

"All three of you will be dead," she snaps.

229

"Either you help me, or I do this on my own. Either way, I'm doing as he says."

She lets out a long breath. "Fine. But for the record, I'm against this."

"Noted."

An hour later, I'm walking out of Kingdom with one of Luca's baseball caps and a hoodie on. I look like an idiot, considering it's summer in Nevada, but I don't want my face being recognized on one of the cameras just in case. I know the Kings are on Luca's side and that Titan does a damn good job with security. The casino is covered in them —interior and exterior—so I gotta cover all my bases.

Walking down the steps, stretched limos and cabs come and go through the circular valet drive. I shove my hands in the pocket of the hoodie and grip my phone. I have it on silent in case I get a phone call, so they won't hear it go off. I need to keep it on me at all times.

A hand grips my right upper arm. "Excuse me ...?"

"He's waiting around the corner for you," the male explains.

My stomach drops. Does he mean the driver or Rossi? I didn't think he would come himself. I go to look up at the man, but he snaps at me. "Keep your head down."

I drop it and take in a shaky breath. All I can do is pray that Jasmine has already called Luca, and he's got Titan checking the surveillance now and they're tracking the app I installed on my phone for her. I tried to think of every possibility for them to find me before I end up dead.

We walk down the sidewalk and sweat drips down my back from the heat of the sun and nervousness. Rounding the corner, I see a black stretch limo looking out of place at the back of an alley. My sweaty hand grips my phone tighter. I wonder if Luca's calling me right now. I put it on silent for a reason. I didn't want to have the urge to answer it once he finds out what I've done. He's going to be so pissed at me. If Rossi doesn't kill me, he probably will.

We come up to the limo, and the guy opens the back door. I just stand there. "Get in," he orders.

"I want to see my mother first," I demand.

He lets out a frustrated growl and shoves me inside.

I slide across the back bench.

"Haven."

I straighten and turn to see Rossi sitting across from me on the other bench with his back to the partition. He has his arms stretched across the top. A large duffel bag sits at his feet. I pray he doesn't plan on stuffing it with my body. My mother sits beside him. Her hands are wrapped in duct tape in front of her and another piece is over her mouth. She's alive, and there's no blood or bruises. I let out a long breath. "Let her go," I order.

He just laughs but doesn't open a door to let her out. My chest tightens at what he plans on doing with her.

My eyes dart around the large space. It's just the three of us until the guy that had my arm crawls in beside me. I scoot to the far side, pressing my back into the door.

The guy goes to reach for me, but Rossi raises his hand. "Let her be."

I let out a shaky breath I didn't know I was holding.

He lifts his right hand and raps his knuckles on the tinted partition. "Drive."

I swallow. "Where are we going?" If he just wanted to talk to me, we could do that right here. He wouldn't need to take me anywhere. Maybe he plans on just going around the block.

His dark eyes look me up and down, and I feel my skin crawl. I hate how much I look like him. How my eyes are the same color and shape. I have his lips and cheekbones. I never saw it before. Of course, I never thought he would be my father. But now that I know, I couldn't deny it even if I wanted to. He told me I looked like my mother, but he was lying. He knows we hold very little resemblance.

"Get undressed."

I blink. "Excuse me?"

"I said get undressed," Rossi repeats.

My mother begins mumbling something behind her tape, but he ignores her.

I stare at him. My heart beating wildly as I'm hoping I misunderstood him both times. I look at the guy next to me. He looks to be around Luca's age, but I don't recognize him. "I ... I don't understand."

Rossi leans forward and unzips the duffel bag, pulling out a white dress. "Luca wants a bride. I'm going to give him one."

My stomach sinks, and tears immediately burn my eyes. I look from my mother to him. "Please ..." I cringe at the sound of my own voice. I've never heard someone sound so desperate.

"I know how much he loves you," he says with disgust. "And I also know how much you love him."

"I don't—"

"Shut up!" he shouts. "You think I don't know that the explosion wasn't an accident? You went to him."

"I didn't!"

The guy who sits next to me backhands me across the face. I cry out, and my mother's muffled scream follows.

The force knocks me to the floor of the limo, and my phone falls out of my pocket. I scramble to get it, but Rossi is faster.

He looks down at it and frowns. "I thought you'd be smarter than this." Reaching over, he cracks the window and throws it out.

The first tear runs down my face. That was the only lifeline I had.

"Don't worry, Haven. He'll know exactly where you are when I'm ready for him to know." With that, he looks at the younger guy. "Help her get undressed."

LUCA

I sit up in my office at Glass when my cell rings. I don't recognize the number but hit answer. "Hello?"

"Luca. It's Jasmine ..." she rushes out.

I jump to my feet. "Everything okay?"

"It's Haven. She went to meet Rossi ..."

"What?" I shout, grabbing my jacket and rushing out the door.

"He called her."

"When?" I run down the stairs outside of the building.

"A little over an hour ago. He had her mom."

Shit!

"He wanted her to meet him outside of Kingdom. He was sending a driver. I downloaded a locating app on her phone for you to track her."

I come to a stop. "Wait. Are you saying you two planned for this to happen?" I demand. My chest almost heaving with my breathing.

"I tried to talk her out of it."

"Jasmine ..."

"She wouldn't even listen to me," she rushes out. I can

hear her panting across the line. Her nervousness giving her away.

Fuck! He'll kill her. After what I did and said today to the reporters, he's on to us. He knows. And she's going to pay for it. "Where the fuck is Nite?" He was supposed to stay with her. He had orders.

"Well ..."

"What did you do, Jasmine?" I start my car and throw it in reverse.

"He's fine. Just asleep."

I shake my head. "Where the fuck are you?"

"Still at Kingdom. In your suite."

"Where is he headed with her?" My car turns sideways in the street as I pull into traffic.

"That's the problem. It's stopped. He must have found it and threw it out."

I hang up on her and call Bones.

TWENTY

HAVEN

"**H**ELP HER OUT," Rossi orders the young man. He grabs my upper arm and yanks me out of the limo and shoves me forward. I look around the area, and fresh tears sting my eyes. The lights of Vegas are miles away. He's brought us to the desert. And that only means one thing. He confirms it a second later.

Opening the trunk, Rossi pulls out a shovel. "Start digging," he orders and throws it at me.

I catch it before letting it drop to my feet. Pulling my shoulders back, I lift my chin. "I won't dig his grave." I refuse to do it.

He gives me a cruel smile as he takes a step closer. "Cute." He grips my chin roughly and jerks my head back. I bite my tongue to keep from crying out at the pain. "This is for you, Haven. I won't let a Rossi be a disgrace to this family."

Is he going to bury me alive? "I'm not a Rossi," I grind out. "I'm a Knowles, you sorry son of a bitch."

He throws his head back, laughing as if I just told a joke. "You are just like me."

"I'm nothing like you," I spit out.

"You are. You're just too stubborn to admit it." He gets in my face. "Your mother was a coward. And Jimmy was a coward. Luca did me a favor by killing that spineless bastard." He shoves me away.

I rub my chin. "Why do you care who I marry?" I demand. "No one knows that I'm yours. Why should it matter about the Rossi name?"

"The Bianchi family has been a pain in my ass for years," he answers. "He stole from me. Embarrassed me. And you marrying his son is his last step at taking over Vegas!" he shouts.

I almost laugh. I hate John Bianchi more than anything, and I refuse to die because of him. Not like this. Not now. "Well, I think you should have done more homework," I say.

"What does that mean?" His dark eyes narrow on me.

"My *father* signed a contract." I hate Jimmy just as much as Rossi does, but I'm going to rub it in his face. I place my left hand out, showing off my ring. "It was a marriage license. I've been a Bianchi for two weeks now. The ceremony was just going to be a formality."

I don't even get to smile in satisfaction at the look of pure rage in his black eyes. He doesn't even allow me a second to take in a breath. His fist hits my face so hard that my head snaps back, and the last thing I hear is him ordering the young guy to put me in the car before the darkness swallows me.

LUCA

"Anything?" I ask Bones as he enters my suite.

He shakes his head. "He must have turned it off before he ditched it."

By the time I got back to Kingdom, Jasmine was in tears and crying on the couch in our hotel suite. The location was gone. And so was my wife.

I run a hand through my hair and remove my suit jacket. It was too hot and the expensive fabric too constricting.

"Thanks," Titan says before hanging up his cell. "James said that he watched her on the monitor, and she got in a limo parked in the back of the alley. He followed it for as long as our cameras would reach, and he ditched the phone just a block down the street. Threw it out the window."

"How many men were in the limo?" I ask him.

"A man was waiting for her outside of Kingdom and walked her to the waiting car. He got in with her. There could have been multiple men inside. The windows were too dark to see."

"Fuck!" I kick the end table by the couch, knocking it over. The glass filled with scotch hits the floor and shatters along with the lamp.

"We'll find her," Grave assures me from behind the bar.

I shake my head. "That's not my fear." Rossi will take me to her, that I know. What I'm afraid of is the condition I'll find her in once he decides to call me.

Jasmine rocks back and forth on the couch, hugging herself while she cries. Nite stands over in a corner trying to come out of whatever Jasmine fed him. I haven't asked and don't care at this point. He will handle that once he fully comes around. Right now, I need to find Haven and save her before it's too late.

I look away from him, but then go back. My mind wanders. Running over to him, I grab his upper arm and pull him into the spare bedroom. "Where did they take you?" I ask him. We never spoke about what happened to him. Not in detail. I knew he was taken from his house and then dropped off at mine. He chose to take a vow of silence, and I honored it until now.

He rubs the back of his neck. "The desert. They tied me up and threw me in a trunk. About an hour later, the car stopped, and they made me dig a grave …"

"Fuck," I hiss.

"It took about thirty minutes. But once I was done, they told me that was where they would bury me if I didn't give them the information they wanted." He clears his throat. "I refused to say a word. That was when they changed their minds and decided to take my tongue instead."

But they were stupid. When they dumped him off at my doorstep, they left his tongue. I made a call and had a doctor meet him immediately to reattach it. They couldn't guarantee full recovery, but Nite beat the odds.

"Do you remember anything about the location?" I ask.

"Not really," he answers. "I was disoriented. They had beat on me pretty hard. It was dark …"

"What about afterward?" I dig.

He shakes his head. "They locked me back in the trunk."

"Maybe—" My cell ringing back in the living room interrupts me. I grab it off the coffee table to see it's a blocked number. "It's him. Stay quiet," I order, then answer, placing it on speakerphone. "Where the fuck is she?"

He laughs. "Well, hello to you too, Luca. Or should I call you *son*?"

My teeth grind. *He knows.* Which puts her life in even more danger. "Cut the shit, Rossi. Where the fuck is she?"

"She's here with me."

I fist my hands. "Where? Let me talk to her."

"She's unavailable at the moment."

"Goddammit—"

"But there's still time," he interrupts me. "I'll send you an address."

"Rossi ..."

He hangs up.

"Fuck!" I go to throw my cell across the room, but Bones grabs my hand.

"You're going to need that." He takes it from me. "Break this." And hands me a glass sculpture that looks like the Eiffel Tower. "We'll get her," he says, nodding his head. "We'll do whatever it takes to get her back. Understood?"

I nod, trying to convince myself when my phone dings in his hand. He looks down at it, and his jaw tightens.

"What is it?" I ask. My heart picking up with adrenaline.

He looks up at me as he shows me the phone. "It's the desert."

———

I DRIVE ABOUT FORTY-FIVE MINUTES OUT OF TOWN. THE sun has started to set, and I know that he did this on purpose. He's had her and her mother for over five hours. He waited this late, knowing that we'd lose daylight. He wants the advantage of knowing the area. And who knows how many guys he has with him. He's either cocky and has no one, or he has an army.

I turn my GPS off. It shows I have a little over two hundred feet left, but I don't need it. I can see the lights from the limo ahead. I take a deep breath as I remove the gun from my shoulder holster. He'll assume I'm carrying, and I want to show him that I'm not armed. I just want her back safe. He can do whatever he wants with me.

I come to a stop and turn off my car, but leave my lights on, needing as much visibility as possible. We'll lose light very soon.

"Where is she?" I ask, slamming the door shut.

He stands there with his arms crossed over his chest and legs spread wide. A guy I know by the name of Donatello stands next to him. I should have killed that fucker that night at the chapel. I take a quick look around. The limo is the only other car out here.

"Pat him down," Rossi orders his man.

I yank on my shirt; the buttons go flying. I shove the shredded material off my shoulders and toss it to the dirt. Throwing up my hands, I turn in a circle so he can see I'm not packing. When I turn back to face him, I demand, "Where the fuck is she?"

He looks over at Donatello and nods.

He walks over to the limo and opens the back door. He bends down, reaching inside, and pulls her out. My chest tightens when I see her. She's wearing a fitted white lace dress that looks like a wedding dress. Her wrists are duct taped behind her back and a piece is over her mouth. Her face has bruises on it and blood runs from her nose, over the tape and onto the once white dress. It's dirty as though she's rolled around in the dirt since she put it on.

"Haven ..." I step toward her.

Rossi pulls his gun out and holds it up at me.

I stop and throw my hands up. "Let her go!" I shout.

"You know, you two are like Romeo and Juliet." He muses with laughter. "And we both know what happened to them."

"Let her go!" I scream at the top of my lungs.

The smile drops off his face. All humor gone. He reaches over, grips her hair, and yanks her to him. She cries out behind the tape. He shoves her to her knees, yanking her head back, then places the gun to her temple.

"Stop! Stop!" He's going to kill her and make me watch. He'll kill me last. He may even let me live a few days after he throws her in the grave that separates us just to make me suffer. "What do you want?" I find myself asking even though I know the answer. I just need to keep him talking while I wait for my backup. They're not far behind me.

"What I want is to shoot you dead, throw you in the grave, and then bury her alive with you!" he shouts. "What I want is for her to suffer for your family's sins."

"What sins?" I demand.

"You know, your father and I were friends once."

"What the fuck does that matter?" I want to run to her, but I'll let him waste time venting about the past.

"We worked together. Had plans to take over Las Vegas. But he took something from me. Something that could never be replaced."

"What?" I ask, taking a quick look at Haven. Her eyes are closed, and tears run down her bloody and dirty face.

"She meant everything to me!" he shouts, getting angry all over again.

"Who was she?" I ask, not believing a damn word he says.

"Ava."

"What?" I ask. That name makes my heart skip a beat. He must be mistaken.

"Ava," he repeats, still holding the barrel to Haven's temple. "I was in love with her. We had been sleeping together when your father took her from me."

He was sleeping with my aunt? "I don't understand ..."

"Your uncle Marco ... He was a conniving little bitch!" he screams. Shaking his head, he yanks Haven's head back even farther, and she whimpers. "And now I'll take a Bianchi ..."

Just then, a light shines on all of us. When he takes the second to look over his shoulder, I pounce, running at him. My shoulder hits his chest, knocking all three of us to the ground. His gun falls to the dirt, and I pick it up, pointing it at Donatello running toward us and fire. He drops dead.

Then I punch Rossi in the face, knocking his ass out cold.

I hear car doors open and close. I ignore them, knowing they're my backup, and storm over to Haven. I rip off the tape that covers her mouth.

"Luca—"

"You okay?" I ask, interrupting her. Gripping her face softly, I look over her bruises and busted lip. It'll all heal. She'll just need some rest and pain meds for a few days. "Does anything feel broken?"

"No," she chokes out, shaking her head.

"Here." I look up to see Titan come over to us. He kneels and cuts her bound wrists with his knife.

"Thank you," she cries, rubbing them. "My mother ..."

"Bones is helping her out of the limo," Titan answers her.

We help her stand, and I push her into him. "Take them both to my car," I say when Bones rounds the back of the limo with a crying Misty. She doesn't have a scratch on her, though.

"No, Luca ..."

I kiss her gently so I don't hurt her busted lip. "It's going to be fine. I promise you. We're almost done."

She nods, letting Titan guide them to my car and get them settled inside. Then he comes to stand next to me.

"Get him ready, Kings," I order.

TWENTY-ONE
ROSSI

Sixteen years ago

"WHAT HAPPENED?" I ask, entering the house.

I find Ava sitting at the kitchen table in her underwear. She holds her face in her hands. "Ava! What in the fuck happened?" I demand, yanking her hands away.

Her brown eyes look up at me with tears running down her face. Makeup smeared all over.

"I didn't know ... what to do ..." She sobs. "Who to call ..."

"I'm here. You did the right thing. What is it?" I ask, pushing her hair back off her face and behind her ear.

"He's in the living room." She bows her head.

I stand and walk into the living room. I see her husband and my best friend, Marco Bianchi, lying in a pool of his own blood. He was shot between his eyes. One bullet. Instant death.

Placing my hand over my mouth, I suck in a deep breath.

SHANTEL TESSIER

What in the fuck? Did she kill him? Is she wanting me to get rid of him? Turning around and rushing back to the kitchen, I find her in the same position I left her.

I grip her hair and yank her head back. "Who the fuck did this?" I demand. She wouldn't have the balls. She also doesn't know much about guns. There's no way she'd be that good of a shot, even if she was standing right in front of him.

She's sobbing uncontrollably. Her bottom lip quivering and body shaking. I don't have time for it. "Who?" I shout, making her flinch.

"John Bianchi. He and Luca showed up ..."

I let go of her and run a hand through my hair. "What did you say?" I growl.

"Nothing."

"Bullshit!" I snap. "You ran your mouth. You had to have. Otherwise, he wouldn't have shot his brother."

Italians are big on family and loyalty. But if they fear someone has stepped out on them, then they put a bullet in your head. They take their code of silence very seriously.

Case in point.

Something more happened tonight that she hasn't told me.

"Tell me," I order.

She looks up at me. Dark eyes wide and red from crying. "I told you I would leave him ..."

"I told you that wasn't an option," I bark out. We've been fucking for over a year now, and she's wanted to leave him for most of that time. But the mafioso doesn't allow divorce. The only way out is death.

She wipes her tear-streaked face, and whispers, "I went to the cops ..."

"Motherfucker!" I hiss.

She jumps to her feet. "I did it for us. I thought if they could convict him, then I'd be free of him. Of this lie."

I reach back and slap her across the face, knocking her back into her seat. She cups her cheek, crying out. I grip her hair and yank her head back. Getting in her face, I growl. "You were just a fuck to me," I lie. "Do you understand that?" I shake her.

"I ... love you," she chokes out.

I can't afford to love her. Not anymore. I understand this life very well. And she just fucked herself. "You are one very stupid woman." She shakes. "You are also a very dead woman." Letting her go, I take a step back.

"Wait," she cries. "Please don't go. I didn't know that John would do this. He wasn't supposed to find out ..."

"You've done this to yourself," I tell her, knowing there is nothing I can do for her. John Bianchi will have her taken out next. He won't do it himself. If so, she'd be dead right now. No, he'll pay someone to do it. And I hate him for it. I hate her for being so fucking stupid. This will ruin more than just her life. My ties to the Bianchi family will be severed. John won't take the chance of getting caught now that she's broken her silence. No wonder the feds are digging around. John will have to pay off the cops. It'll cost him. It'll cost all of us.

"Rossi, please ..."

"They'll come for you," I tell her. "The best thing you can do is run." Then I turn and leave her.

I walk down the steps to her house and get into my car. Pulling out my cell, I call up John.

"Hello?"

"You killed your brother?" I growl.

"Yes. I saved both of our asses," he answers. "Whatever they have on me, they have on you as well."

"And Ava?" I question, needing to hear him say it.

"It must be done," he says.

"Bianchi ..."

"You are the one who fell in love with a snitch, Rossi. Let Marco's body be a warning of what happens to those who forget their place in this world." Click.

TWENTY-TWO

LUCA

I WATCH ROSSI stir in the dirt. He lets out a moan and tries to move. "What ...?" he questions, opening his eyes.

"What was your favorite game to play in school?" I ask the Kings.

"Tug of war," Titan answers. "I always loved when a kid challenged me to rip his arms off. Literally."

"What the fuck, Luca?" Rossi demands, now coherent. He fights the restraints around his arms and ankles.

I kneel beside him. "Thank you for digging that grave. It's going to save me a lot of time."

"Luca ..."

I stand and place my fingers in my mouth, letting out a whistle, signaling Grave and Cross we're ready to go.

The engine to the limo and Bones's car come to life, and they place them both in drive. The chains wrapped around Rossi's bound wrists and ankles pull tight.

He throws his head back, grinding his teeth as the Kings slowly begin to drive away from one another.

While he was passed out, we secured the chains around

him and connected them to the bumpers of the cars. We are going to rip him in half.

"LUCA!" he screams as the seams of his shirt rip under his arms. His body pulled so taut it lifts inches off the desert ground. "Argh," he grounds out. His face turns red, and his shirt rides up, showing off his stomach. You can see the skin pulled so tight it's white as a ghost. Ready to split.

He tries to take a deep breath, but he can't. The cars hold him at a standstill. Neither one moving any farther. I give a nod, and they hit the gas. It rips his body in half. Blood squirts everywhere, and his insides fall out. Both parts of his body being dragged away by the cars.

Titan hits me on the back, and I smile. One sorry bastard down. I don't care who he was. He can't hurt my wife anymore.

The cars come to a stop, and I walk over to his torso and head. I unhook the chain from the bumper and drag his ass over to the grave and kick it in. Bones repeats the process with his lower half. Grave, Cross, and I grab the extra shovels we brought and start throwing dirt over his body parts, knowing he'll never be found out here.

There has always been a misconception about the Nevada desert. Some say that it's too hard to bury bodies out here. Those would be the people too lazy to dig. It's doable. I've done it plenty of times. And I know this isn't the Dark Kings' first body they've thrown dirt on. Just depends on how hard you're willing to work to hide your evidence.

EPILOGUE

HAVEN

S ITTING AT THE bridal table in the front of the ballroom, I take a sip of my champagne as I gaze at everyone. I catch sight of Luca sitting at a table over to the left. Forearms resting on the white tablecloth, he's leaning forward, talking to Titan and Bones who sit across from him. Titan's jaw clenches, and his hands fist at whatever my husband is saying.

I smile. *Husband*. We're married. Well, technically we have been married, but now the world knows. It wasn't the ceremony that Luca and his father had originally planned. It went from four hundred guests to fifty. And it was perfect. The Kings were nice enough to give us the ballroom on the fiftieth floor of Kingdom. And we chose an evening ceremony because I love the way the city lights up at night. It's at the corner of the tower so you can see most of the Strip from the floor-to-ceiling windows.

I look away from them to the back of the room and see Jasmine step into the ballroom. She has her head down, and her red hair covers her face. She places one hand the white column wrapped in red roses and her other hand on her heaving chest. She looks up, and her face is flushed. Her lips parted. She looks like she's having a heart attack. I start to stand to go to her, but I stop when I see Nite walk up next to her. He places his hand on her back while taking her other hand in his. He helps her to the nearest table, pulls out a chair, and has her sit in it.

As if he feels my eyes on him, he looks up at me. I frown, looking from her to him. Then the corner of his lips curves up, and I realize what's going on. They just had sex. At my wedding. I chuckle. Good for her.

Finishing my champagne, I look at the empty glass and smile to myself. For as much as it's a great day, it's also sad. Two very important people aren't here.

Emilee and Mia.

I unzip my clutch and pull out my cell. I go to Mia's number and send her a quick text.

> Me: I wish you were here.

> Mia: Me too. Maybe I'll see you soon.
> Congratulations on the wedding. And
> welcome to the family. Sister.

I think about that message. Luca and I are supposed to be going to Fiji tomorrow morning, but I don't see why we can't stop in Italy first.

Everyone is still mingling and drinking. My husband is still in a heated discussion with Bones and Titan. Grave and Cross are nowhere to be seen, and Jasmine has disappeared again. Round two?

I get up from the table, slip through the back door that leads to the elevator, and walk down the hallway to the end. Looking out the window at Sin City, I hit call.

"You've reached Emilee. Sorry I missed your call ..."

250

Straight to voicemail. I let out a sigh and listen to her recording until it beeps. "Hey, E. I've been trying to call you. I ... I miss you. And wish you were here. Jasmine told me you're moving back. You better call me as soon as you set foot off that plane. We need to have a girls' night. Drink too much and eat more chicken wings than our stomachs can handle." I laugh. "I just ... I just wanted to tell you that I miss and love you." I hang up and turn around to head back, but I pause when I see the door close softly. I frown. Was someone listening to my conversation?

LUCA

I WATCH AS Haven re-enters the ballroom from the hallway. She places her phone down on the bridal table and walks over to the bar where her mother stands talking to Titan.

"Hello?" Bones answers his cell as he sits across from me at a table. He nods once to himself. "Titan and I will be there first thing in the morning, and we'll discuss it then." He hangs up.

"Problem?" I ask.

Leaning back in the chair, he laces his fingers behind his head. "Looks like someone doesn't wanna pay us what they owe."

"Who is it?" Las Vegas is small. It may be some big fancy city to a cowboy from Lawton, Oklahoma, but trust me, it's not.

"George Wilton."

My brows rise. "George Wilton as in York and Wilton Construction?"

He nods, putting his arms down, and begins to undo his tie like it's choking him.

"As in Nick York?" I clarify, making sure I understand. His jaw clenches.

That's Emilee's father. "They owe you money?"

"Not Nick. Only George."

"Well ... that's—"

"Unfortunate for him," he interrupts me.

I scratch the back of my head. "How much?"

"Five hundred thousand."

I snort. "That's chump change to you."

"It is. But if I let every piece of shit who owes Kingdom money get away with it, then Kingdom would be no more."

"True."

"Titan and I did some research before we loaned him the money to make sure he was good for it. And he was, but everything having to do with the company is in Nick's name."

"Well, that makes sense. Nick came from money." His dad was a billionaire. So was his grandfather. That oil money goes a long way. "What about Wilton?" He was raised by a single mother and grew up in Section 8 housing. He got a scholarship for football, and that's where he met Nick York. They became best friends, and after graduation, they started a company together. Of course, Nick backed the entire thing. "You could blackmail him ... The company ..."

"I don't want that company." He waves me off. "York's a good man. From what I remember anyway. Wilton signed that he would repay what he borrowed, so I will hold him personally responsible to pay that back."

"Am I interrupting?"

I look up to see my wife standing next to me. Her hands on her hips of her white wedding dress. It's strapless and form fitting down to her knees where it flares out. I heard

Jasmine call it a mermaid style dress. I don't give a fuck what kind it is; she looks absolutely beautiful in it. And I can't wait to get her out of it.

I scoot my chair back and pat my thigh, gesturing her to have a seat.

She plops down and looks across at Bones. "You don't look happy."

He shakes his head and throws back what's in his glass before standing and walking over to the bar for more.

"Everything okay?" She looks down at me.

"Of course." I wrap my arms around her small waist.

She lays her head on my shoulder, and I look across the ballroom to where Bones stands next to Titan. Haven's mom has moved on to talk with Jasmine, who keeps running her hands through her hair like it's tangled. My eyes go back to the Kings. Bones leans forward and says something to Titan, and he pulls away with a nod. Then they both start to head back over to our table with full drinks.

"Hey ..." Haven sits up and turns to face me. "Can we go to Italy?" Her amber eyes dart around really quickly, and her voice drops. "To see Mia. I really want to spend some time with her. Get to know her better. She is family now."

I cup her face. "Whatever you want." Then I lean forward, placing a soft kiss to her lips.

She pats my chest. "I love you."

Gently gripping her chin, I lean in and kiss her painted red lips softly. "I love you too, Haven."

"Gross. Take it to a room," Titan says, sitting back down in his seat.

She looks over at him and smiles. "I can't wait to watch a King fall." Then she gets up and walks off.

He laughs at that like it was funny as Bones shakes his

head. They start to fill me in on their current situation with George Wilton, but I tune them out.

Leaning back, I watch my wife sit down at the bridal table, and her mom takes my seat next to her. Jasmine leans over the table, and her mouth is running a mile a minute as she tells them a story about something that involves her boobs because she keeps gesturing to them.

I smile and take a drink from my glass. Haven Nicole Knowles belongs to me. Forever. Till death do us part. Which in the life I live, could very well be tomorrow.

The End

THANK YOU FOR TAKING THE TIME TO READ **CODE OF Silence.** Did you enjoy the Dark Kings? Read on for the prologue from **Titan: The Dark Kingdom**

WANT TO KNOW MORE ABOUT *THE DARK KINGDOM Series?*

TITAN

THE DARK KINGDOM

TITAN

I SIT BEHIND my desk, the dark curtains pulled closed to block out the early morning rays of the Las Vegas skyline. Taking a sip of my black coffee, I look up at the five women standing in my office. "Strip down to your bra and underwear," I order.

Four of them begin undressing without hesitation. They do this for a living, though it's usually under flashing lights, fog machines, and thundering music. And don't forget the money that comes with selling your body. But still, they're not shy. The last one on the right watches the others with wide green eyes as she nibbles on her bottom lip.

"Problem?" I ask.

She looks at me and swallows. "I ... uh, I didn't know ... I didn't wear a—"

"You don't have anything I haven't already seen," I interrupt her rambling.

"Here," Sandy chirps. "You can wear mine." She unclasps her black lace bra and holds it out to the blonde. Her rather new and perky looking paid for DDs are now fully on display.

"My boobs are too small for that!" the girl shrieks in horror.

Sandy drops it to the floor and shrugs. She slaps her palms down on her bare thighs and does a little hop in her six-inch heels.

Fuck! It's too early for this shit. I'm not a cheer coach gearing them up for a game. Rubbing my temples, I stare down at their paperwork that covers my black desk. "Megan, you didn't list what your limits are," I announce, glaring up at her through my lashes.

Her eyes drop to the floor, and I don't miss the fact that she's still dressed. Her arms now hugging her small chest. "I didn't understand ..."

"What a limit is?" I bark out.

She flinches and whispers, "I've never done anal ..."

Jesus!

The other girls laugh. "It's more than just that," Sandy tells her with a smile on her face.

"What else could there be?" Megan asks wide-eyed.

Fuck me! This girl is sheltered, and I should have stayed in bed.

"Are you willing to do bondage?" Sandy fills her in, placing her hands on her wide hips "And if so, do you mind being gagged, flogged?" Megan gasps. "If you enjoy being tied up, do you prefer rope, handcuffs, chains." The girl begins to tremble. "There's also fisting ..."

Just then, my office door swings open, and the only woman I don't mind seeing enters my office.

I stand. "Ladies, this is GiGi. Think of her as your ... house mom." Good enough. "She will take your measurements and record them for your files." The four half-naked women nod with excitement. "Once the fitting is over, Dr. Lane will see you."

"Doctor?" Megan swallows.

"Yes." Growling, I look at her. Has she not listened to a damn thing I've said? "All Queens are required to be on birth control. Ninety-five percent of our clients already have wives and children. They want to be guaranteed that there won't be any surprise babies or a client trying to get knocked up for blackmail money." We guarantee our clients' satisfaction. And unplanned pregnancies are not going to obtain that. And I'm not about to trust any woman with my reputation and dedication with my clients.

They all turn and bounce out. "Megan, have a seat." I stop her.

She falls into one of the black leather chairs in front of my desk and looks up at me. Jesus, she has tears in her eyes.

I walk around my desk and lean up against it. "Why are you here?" I ask. Crossing my arms over my chest, I glare down at her.

She picks at a piece of nonexistent lint on her jeans. Her dirty blond hair shields her face from me. "I need money."

No surprise there. "What do you need money for?"

She heaves a heavy sigh, unable to meet my eyes. "My father is a druggie. My mother left us a year ago. Went to the store to buy a pack of cigarettes and never returned." She swallows. "I have a younger brother who's three. I want to get him away from our father, but I don't have that kind of cash. Not to give him what he needs."

"Your application stated that you're twenty-one."

"I lied," she whispers.

I already knew that. And I'm pretty sure she's a goddamn virgin. "How old are you?"

"Eighteen."

"Attending high school?"

She shakes her head. "I dropped out when my brother was born. I needed to stay home with him."

I run a hand down my face, that headache intensifying. "Being a queen isn't a good fit for you." That's as nicely as I can put it.

Her head snaps up. Her green eyes narrow on me before she averts them and slumps her shoulders. "I know. I don't know what I was thinking." She pushes her hair behind her ear.

All types of women come and go from my office, and I can tell when someone is being neglected. Her cheeks are sunken in. Her eyes have circles under them. Her tank top keeps falling off her shoulders, and her collarbones are prominent. She probably makes sure her brother is fed before herself, and I respect that. "Are you quick on your feet?"

She nods once. "And I'm a fast learner.

"Have you ever been a waitress?"

"No."

I sigh. Just let her leave ...

"But I can do it." She sits up straighter, eyes wide with hope. She doesn't wanna take her clothes off, but she's willing to carry drinks around in a tight mini skirt and halter top. Doesn't matter how you dress it up, sex equals money. The more you show, the more you'll make.

Maybe it's my fucking headache, or maybe I'm just in a giving mood. Doubtful, but I say, "Go to this address and give this to Mitch." I walk around my desk and sit down in my chair. I write as I speak. "Tell him I sent you, and he'll get you on the schedule." I tear off the Post-It and reach across the mahogany surface. She can't work in Kingdom. In the state of Nevada, you have to be at least twenty-one to even serve drinks. But I have hookups all over this town, including restaurants.

She grabs the note. "Thank you, Titan. Thank you so much."

I nod and hold up the paperwork. "I'll tear this up except for the NDA." She nods quickly. "What happened up here does not leave this room."

"Yes, sir."

I point at the door. "Get going."

She runs out of my office much faster than she had entered.

Opening the bottom drawer in my desk, I pop the top off the pill bottle and toss a couple into my mouth before washing them down with my coffee.

The girls re-enter my office with GiGi. "All done, Titan." The sixty-five-year-old lady smiles at me. She wears her bleach blond hair up in a tight bun. It's not even eight a.m., and she has a full face of makeup on topped off with fake eyelashes and red painted lips. She's always well put together and in a good mood.

The girls giggle, and Sandy picks up her bra and places her tits back in it.

"Thanks, GiGi. Send Dr. Lane in, will ya?"

She nods.

Sitting back in my chair, I fold my inked arms across my chest and look at the four women who stand before me.

The Queens of Kingdom.

Three of my best friends and I own a hotel and casino in the heart of Las Vegas. I oversee the Queens, our secret service. I have a list of men a mile long who want our girls. A couple of senators, a handful of movie stars, and even more rock stars. CEOs and some blue-collar hardworking dads who just want to blow off some steam before going home to their nagging wife and kids. They fly in from all around the world.

They want a date for a work event, they call me. They want a woman to take on a trip to Maui, they call me. They want a woman for the night in one of our exclusive suites here at Kingdom, they call me.

I pull four cells out of my top drawer. "Here are your phones." I place them on the desk.

They had to hand them over when they arrived earlier. "I downloaded the Queens app on them. If at any time you feel uncomfortable or think it's getting out of hand, make the call. It calls me directly."

The brunette who hasn't said much over the past two hours looks at me. Her name on the NDA she signed says Maggie. She came with Sandy. "Do you have to end a date early often?"

I shake my head. "No. Our clients understand how it works, but I understand that sometimes things can go too far. You have too many drinks. He decides he wants more than what he pays for. You call me, and I'll take care of it."

"Have you had to do it before?"

I nod.

"And?" she asks.

"And I ended it." Simple as that. A girl has never been raped or beaten while on the clock. My clients understand what they sign when they request a girl. If they so much break any rule on the contract, I will break their fucking necks. But I understand I can't be there with them a hundred percent of the time, so we make sure all bases are covered.

For the most part, everything always goes smoothly. The girls get to keep sixty percent of what I charge, and some have never even taken their clothes off. Getting naked and sucking dick aren't required to be a queen, but if that's what they want to do, then by all means. Plus, they get to keep a hundred percent of their tips off the books. That's between the client and the Queen to negotiate.

The cheerful blonde who answered every question on her application with hearts over her i's steps forward. Her name is Whitney. She places her hands on my desk and smiles down at me. I already know where this is going to go. "Do you sample the product? You know, rate it for your clients?"

"No." I don't shit where I work. The Kings and I have enough problems as it is. I don't need to add pussy to the mix.

She pushes her bottom lip out as her dark eyes roam over my inked arms. "That's too bad."

WANT TO DIVE INTO THE LORDS WORLD?

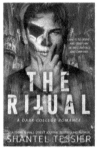

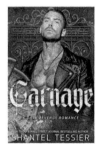

CONTACT ME

Facebook Reader Group: Shantel's Sinful Side

Goodreads: Shantel Tessier

Instagram: shantel_tessierauthor

Website: Shanteltessier.com

Facebook Page: Shantel Tessier Author

TikTok: shantel_tessier_author

Store: shanteltessierstore.com

Shantel Tessier's Spoiler Room. Please note that I have one spoiler room for all books, and you may come across spoilers from book(s) you have not had the chance to read yet. You must answer both questions in order to be approved.